Silly and Stinky Stories

my Grandpa Tells

Jerry E. Hines is retired after working for thirty-five years with the Saint Paul Public Schools. He resides in White Bear Lake, Minnesota, and currently works part time in a local school district with early childhood special needs students. Having three children and three grandchildren helped inspire him to write this book.

Silly and Stinky Stories
my Grandpa Tells

To: Bill ← The only one I'll never pay!!

Hines

Jerry E Hines

AMBER SKYE
PUBLISHING

ISBN: 978-0-9831839-1-4

Library of Congress Catalog Number: 2011937510

Printed in the United States of America

First Printing: September 2011

15 14 13 12 11 5 4 3 2 1

Edited by Kellie M. Hultgren

Illustrations by Simon Goodway

Book Designed by Christopher Fayers

1935 BERKSHIRE DRIVE
EAGAN, MINNESOTA 55122

AMBER SKYE   651.452.0463
PUBLISHING   WWW.AMBERSKYEPUBLISHING.COM

To order, visit www.ItascaBooks.com or www.jerryehines.com or call 1-800-901-3480. Reseller discounts available.

Contents

Dedication

To my three wonderful grandchildren
Cole, Luke, and Tate. Especially Luke,
for his part in making this book come true.

Me and my Grandpa

My name is Luke, and I kind of like to write about stuff, as long as it isn't homework. Someday, I think I'd like to write a book, but not just yet since I'm only eleven years old. I'm pretty sure you need to be older than eleven to write a whole book. Anyway, I decided to write down a bunch of my grandpa's stories and other things that my grandpa and my brother and I did that turned out to be pretty funny. Well, me and my brother . . . (I mean "my brother and I." My mom always corrects me when I say "me and my friend, or me and Jonny, or me and my brother." She says it's not proper English, so I guess I'd better get it right now cuz, if my mom reads this, she'll make me change it for sure.) Anyway, my brother and I thought they were pretty funny—except for the time my brother got hit in the gonads with a tennis ball. He didn't think that was funny. I figure if I write down all this stuff now, then someday maybe I can turn it into a real book.

Like I said, I'm eleven years old. I'm not very big for my age. In fact, I'm actually kind of small. My grandpa says I'm no bigger than a turd, but when I asked him how big he was when he was my age, he said he was even smaller than me. I wanted to ask him if that meant he was just a little turd, but I didn't cuz I didn't want him to think I was a smart aleck.

This year, when I go back to school, I'll be in sixth grade. That means I'll be in middle school instead of elementary school. I'm pretty excited about that cuz I'll have lots of different teachers instead of the same old one, all day long, like in elementary school. My teacher last year, Mr. Palmer, was really boring. In fact, he was so boring that most of the time I could hardly stay awake in his class. It's a good thing I sat in the back of the class so he couldn't see me falling asleep all the time.

I told my grandpa about Mr. Palmer, and he said, "I had a teacher that was even more boring than that when I was in ninth grade. The teacher's name was Mr. Dorring, but all the kids called him Mr. Boring. He was so boring that almost everyone in the class dozed off at one time or another. Mr. Boring would walk around the classroom with a big, old, long, round stick, just waiting for someone to fall asleep. The stick was supposed to be for pointing at stuff on the board, but he used it for poking kids that were messing around."

"Did you ever mess around in class, Grandpa?" I tried to imagine my grandpa putting a note on a friend's back that said "I'M STUPID" or throwing spitballs at kids like I sometimes do.

"Not very much in that class. Most of the time, I would just doze off in Mr. Boring's class. One day, I put my head down on my desk and fell sound asleep. When Mr. Boring walked by my desk and saw me sleeping, he swung that big, old stick and hit my desk right next to my ear. It made a really loud banging noise and scared the bejeebers out of me. It scared me so much I almost wet my pants. In fact, I was still shaking in my fifth-hour wood shop class. Every time I tried to pound a nail into my dumb, little bird house, I hit my finger with the hammer. By the time I finished that bird house, it had seven bent nails sticking out of it which is probably why I got a 'D' on that project."

Since the stories I'm going to write about are mostly my grandpa's stories, I should tell you a little bit about him. First, he doesn't seem like a grandpa cuz of all the stuff that he does. He plays tennis and racquetball and rides his bike and goes swimming and runs almost every day—stuff like that.

A couple of years ago, he asked me and my brother if we wanted to ride our bikes around the lake with him. It's about twelve miles around the lake. When he came to get us, he didn't have his bike so we asked him where it was.

He said, "Oh, I forgot to tell you, I'm going to run while you guys bike."

"You're going to run all the way around the lake?" I asked. "No way!"

"Don't worry," he said. "If I get tired, you can run, and I'll ride your bike."

He never did have to ride my bike. I wonder if I'll be able to run twelve miles when I get to be his age. Oh, yeah, his age is another reason he doesn't seem like a grandpa. I'm not sure how old he is, cuz he never wants to celebrate his birthday, and he won't tell us his real age.

I asked him why he doesn't like to celebrate his birthday and he said, "Because birthdays just remind me that I'm getting older, and I don't like to be reminded about that."

"But if you don't celebrate your birthday, you won't get any presents," I protested.

He laughed, "Presents! Who cares about presents? When you get to be my age, all you ever get is socks and underwear anyway."

The third reason is the real reason that he doesn't seem like a grandpa. It's cuz of all the crazy ideas he comes up with. His ideas may be pretty crazy, but my brother and I think they're actually pretty cool.

Sneaking Out

One of the hardest things about writing stuff that isn't homework is you never know where to start. If our teacher gives us a writing assignment for homework, she tells us what we have to write about. Now that I've decided to do my own writing, I have to figure out what to write and when to write it. I guess that's one of the hard parts about writing on my own. I'll start with something that happened a little while ago.

This happened to me and my brother, Cole, a couple of weeks ago. It's one of my grandpa's crazy ideas that Cole and I thought was cool but our mom and dad didn't.

Cole is two years older than me. That makes him my older brother, but he doesn't always act like it. Sometimes he can act pretty stupid. His real name is Colden, but everyone calls him Cole, except sometimes my mom and dad call him Colden when they're mad. One time Mom was mad at him cuz he left his dirty socks on the kitchen table. They must have been pretty gross smelling cuz my mom wouldn't even touch them.

She came out on the front porch and hollered, "Colden! Get in here!" Then she went back in the house.

Here's the part where he acted pretty dumb. Cole kept playing with us in the front yard and didn't go in the house. I said, "You better go in before you get in trouble."

"She wasn't talking to me," he said. "My name is Cole." And he just kept on playing with us.

After a couple of minutes, my mom came back out, and you could tell she was really mad cuz her face was all red and her eyes were little tiny slits. She had her hands on her hips, which is always a pretty good sign someone is going to get hollered at. My friends Ben and Jonny must have picked up on the signs, too, cuz they both slowly walked out into the street like they were going home.

She walked all the way out into the yard this time and said, "Colden Kenneth, you get your butt in this house right now. Do you hear me?" Cole tried to say something, but she cut him off. "I don't want to hear it, Colden. Just get in the house before I come over there and pull you in the house by your ear."

I don't know what my mom said to him or what happened when he got in the house. All I know is he didn't get to come back out and play. Sometimes my brother just isn't very smart.

Anyway, what was I talking about? Oh, yeah. One hot

summer day, my grandpa and my brother and I rode our bikes down to the beach for a swim. We had a great time like we always do. My grandpa picks us up and throws us in the water and makes us do back flips and stuff like that. On the way home, my grandpa came up with his crazy idea.

"Tomorrow we should get up real early, while your mom and dad are still sleeping, and ride our bikes to McDonald's for breakfast."

My brother and I both said, "Good idea, Grandpa!" and asked him what time he wanted to go.

Grandpa said he would be there at seven o'clock sharp.

"SEVEN O'CLOCK! That's too early," I said. "How are we supposed to get up that early? My mom and dad don't get up until after eight on weekends."

Then Grandpa told us his plan. This is the crazy part. He said he would ride his bike over to our house at seven and throw sticks at Cole's window to wake him up. Then Cole would sneak downstairs and let Grandpa in the house, and they would both come into my bedroom and wake me up. Then we would write a note to my mom and dad, telling them what we were going to do. That way we wouldn't get in trouble.

Well, the plan didn't work very well. Grandpa got to our house at seven o'clock just like he said he would and threw sticks at my brother's window, but my brother never woke up. Grandpa kept hollering and throwing sticks at the window for about fifteen minutes. Finally, all the noise woke up my dad, and he went downstairs to let Grandpa in.

Then my grandpa came up to our rooms and woke us up.

My dad was pretty mad at Grandpa for waking him up so early on a Saturday morning. Grandpa was pretty mad at Cole for not waking up when the sticks hit his window. At least nobody was mad at me. I don't think my grandpa was really mad at Cole cuz we were laughing and joking about it all the way to McDonalds, but I'm pretty sure my dad was really mad at Grandpa.

On the way home, Grandpa thought of a new way he could wake up Cole instead of throwing sticks at the window. He said his new plan couldn't fail. All the way home we kept bugging Grandpa to tell us about it, but he wouldn't. He just said, "Don't worry. You'll see soon enough."

When we got home, we went up to Cole's bedroom. Grandpa opened the door and, when he looked inside, shook his head. "HOLY MOLY ROCKY!" (That's one of his favorite sayings.) "Don't you ever clean your bedroom?"

Cole laughed and turned a little red. "Yeah, but only when my mom makes me. I'll bet your bedroom looked like this when you were my age, Grandpa."

"Nope," Grandpa said, "It looked even worse. But that was because we had five of us in one bedroom."

"FIVE!" Cole and I looked at each other. "No way!"

"That's right, five. There were nine kids in the family, and we only had two bedrooms, so all the boys had to sleep in one bedroom."

"How could five kids sleep in one bedroom?" I asked. "You must have had three bunk beds."

"They didn't have bunk beds when I was a kid. We had two regular-sized beds like yours. My brother David and I slept in one, and Ray and Roger slept in the other. My brother Jim was the oldest, so he got to sleep in a little bed by himself."

"Three beds in one room. Man, there must not have been room for anything else. Where did you keep all your toys?"

"We didn't have many toys, but the ones we did have we stuffed under our beds with all the dirty clothes . . . just like you do."

My brother and I started laughing, and then my grandpa told us something we thought was even funnier. "The worst part about having so many of us in one room was we had to share our underwear."

"Share your underwear? No way!" We laughed so hard we got tears in our eyes.

I pictured my grandpa and his brother stumbling around, trying to get into the same pair of underwear. Then Grandpa explained what he meant.

"Yup, there was just enough room, next to my brother's bed, for one dresser. It had three drawers in it, and that's where we kept all of our clothes. The bottom drawer was the biggest, and that's where everybody's pants were. The middle drawer had everybody's shirts, and the top drawer was the smallest, where we kept all of our socks and underwear.

"When our mom did the wash, she would dump a basketful of underwear on one of the beds and tell us we had to sort them out. They were tighty whities, so they all looked the same. We weren't about to try and figure out whose underwear was whose, so we just picked up the whole pile and dumped it in the top drawer with the socks. Whoever needed a pair first got to pick first. That's why you could say we just shared our underwear."

When Cole and I stopped laughing, I said, "Did you ever end up wearing your sister's underwear by mistake?" That made my brother laugh even harder, but Grandpa just shook his head.

Finally, my grandpa told us about his plan to make sure Cole woke up the next time he came to get us for breakfast. He asked Cole if he had any string in his bedroom. Cole didn't think so, but we looked through all the junk in his room anyway. Then I remembered a kite that I had stuck in the back of my closet. I went to my room, found the ball of kite string, and brought it to Grandpa.

"Here, Grandpa. But how is a ball of string going to wake up Cole?"

"You'll see in a minute," he said, as he started to unwind the string and spread it around the room.

He tied a small pencil on one end of the string, draped it over the curtain rod and opened the window. Next he unfastened the screen on one side and slid the pencil out the window. He lowered the pencil so it was hanging just above the garage door.

Cole and I looked at Grandpa and shrugged our shoulders. We had no idea how the piece of string with a pencil tied to it could possibly wake up Cole.

"There," Grandpa said. "Now all you have to do is take this end of the string and tie it to your toe when you go to bed. When I get here in the morning, I'll grab a hold of the pencil and tug on the string until it wakes you up."

Both Cole and I said, "COOL!" at the same time. Cole took off his sock, crawled into his bed and tied the string to his big toe. "Grandpa, go outside and pull on the string so we can see if it works."

Grandpa went outside and pulled on the string. Sure enough, Cole could feel the string tugging away at his toe. All we had to do now was wait 'til morning to see if it *really* worked.

On Saturday morning, Grandpa rode his bike to our house at seven o'clock, just like he said he would. He tugged on the string once, but nothing happened. He tugged on the string again, only harder and quite a few times. All of a sudden, there was a loud scream. It was Cole.

A few seconds later, my dad was in Cole's room, trying to find out what all the screaming was about. I heard Cole say that he thought something was under his covers biting his foot. He had forgotten that he had tied the string to his toe, and each time Grandpa pulled on the string, it lifted Cole's covers and hurt his toe. My dad turned on the light and saw the string. He followed it to the window and looked outside. There was my grandpa, standing in the driveway, looking up at the window.

He was mad at Cole for waking up the whole

neighborhood and mad at Grandpa for his stupid idea, and Grandpa was mad at Cole for getting him in trouble with my dad. And me . . . well, once again, nobody was mad at me. And that was the last time Grandpa rode his bike to our house on a Saturday morning to take us out for breakfast without asking our dad first.

The Life Saver Fairy

When I was just a little kid, I believed in the Tooth Fairy. I'm pretty sure almost every kid probably did, cuz if they didn't then they wouldn't get any money for their teeth. The last time I put a tooth under my pillow, I got a dollar for it; but my friend Ben got five dollars for his tooth. So I asked my grandpa how come the Tooth Fairy gave Ben five dollars and she only gave me one dollar. My grandpa told me it was cuz I had bad breath and Ben probably didn't. He said bad breath makes your teeth stink, and the Tooth Fairy doesn't like stinky teeth, so she doesn't give as much money for them.

I thought about that for a while, and then told my grandpa that my dad must have had really bad breath when he was a kid cuz he told me he only got a dime for each of his teeth.

Anyway, I'm too old to believe in the Tooth Fairy anymore, but I definitely believe in the Life Saver Fairy. If you've never heard of the Life Saver Fairy, she's the one who goes around and leaves a Life Saver—you know, the Life Savers candy—in your shoe or under your pillow or in your pocket or somewhere in your bed or in some other weird place when you least expect it.

The first time I found out about the Life Saver Fairy was after one of my soccer games. When I took off my soccer shoes and put on my tennis shoes, I felt something in one of them and thought it was a rock. I took off the shoe to get the rock out and found out it wasn't a rock at all, it was a cherry Life Saver. For a minute, I wondered how a Life Saver could get in my tennis shoe out there in the middle of a soccer field. Then I looked over at my grandpa, and he was kind of smiling at me, so I figured he must have put it there.

"Hey, Grandpa, thanks for the Life Saver," I said.

He walked over and asked, "What Life Saver? I didn't give you a Life Saver."

"Grandpa, I know you did. You must have put it in my tennis shoe when I was playing soccer."

"Not me," he said, "It must have been the Life Saver Fairy."

"Yeah, sure, Grandpa, the Life Saver Fairy. Right! There's no such thing as a Life Saver Fairy." I figured my grandpa was coming up with another one of his stories.

My grandpa sat down next to me. "You mean to tell me you've never heard of the Life Saver Fairy? That's too bad, because kids who don't believe in the Life Saver Fairy miss out on getting Life Savers throughout their entire lives. The Life Saver Fairy must have thought you believed in him or her or whatever it is, or else she wouldn't have left you a Life Saver."

He pushed me over as I was trying to tie my shoe. "All I know for sure is this," he said, "If you don't say thank you to the Life Saver Fairy, she'll probably never visit you again. Oh, and you have to say it pretty loud, because the Life Saver Fairy can't hear very well."

Sure enough, my grandpa had come up with another goofy idea. So, just to be funny, I decided to yell my thank you as loud as I could. I wanted to see if it would embarrass my grandpa.

"THANK YOU, LIFE SAVER FAIRY!" I screamed at the top of my lungs.

All the people at the game turned around and looked at me like I was crazy. The only person it didn't bother was my grandpa—it didn't bother him one bit. He just laughed.

Then my mom came over and said, "Lucas John! What is the matter with you?" She only calls me Lucas John when she's mad. I tried to explain that Grandpa said I had to thank the Life Saver Fairy or else the Life Saver Fairy wouldn't ever give me another Life Saver. She just rolled her eyes and said, "I should have known this would have something to do with your grandpa."

I got up and went over to my soccer bag to put away my shoes, and when I bent over to open my bag, I noticed there was another Life Saver on top of the bag. My Grandpa was still sitting where I left him. I couldn't figure out how he could have put the Life Saver on my soccer bag when he was sitting with me. Now I was seriously beginning to wonder, was there really such a thing as a Life Saver Fairy? I figured, from now on, I'd better always thank the Life Saver Fairy . . . no matter what.

When I got home, I told my brother about the Life Saver Fairy and how Grandpa said that, if you didn't thank her, she probably wouldn't ever visit you again. My brother just laughed.

A couple of weeks later, the Life Saver Fairy came to one of Cole's baseball games and left a Life Saver in one of *his* shoes. The coach was talking to the team at the end of the game, but my brother wasn't paying attention. When he found the Life Saver, he remembered what I had told him, then looked at my grandpa and hollered, "THANKS, LIFE SAVER FAIRY!"

The team looked at him like he was crazy, and my dad turned all red in the face and got mad, but my brother didn't care. He knew that, if he didn't thank the Life Saver Fairy, she'd never come back. But my brother didn't think it was too funny when the coach made him take a couple of laps around the field for not paying attention while he was talking.

The Life Saver Fairy kept coming back. Once I found one in my jacket pocket when my grandpa wasn't even with me. Another time my brother found one in his ice skates after a hockey practice and Grandpa wasn't there either.

Cole said, "I skated the whole time with the Life Saver in my skate and didn't realize it until the end of practice."

"Did you eat it?" I asked.

"Sure I ate it. Why wouldn't I?"

"It must have tasted like a stinky old sock."

"Nope, it just tasted like a sweaty cherry lifesaver."

One time my grandpa brought me and my friend Ben home from a soccer game. Ben knew about the Life Saver Fairy, so when he found a Life Saver in his shoe, he knew what he had to do. Ben waited until we dropped him off in his driveway before he thanked the Life Saver Fairy. As we were pulling out of his driveway, Ben started yelling, "THANK YOU, LIFE SAVER FAIRY!" at the top of his lungs. He kept on shouting it while my grandpa and I drove down the street. We thought it was pretty funny, but the next time I saw Ben, he told me his dad didn't think it was very funny at all. I guess not everyone likes the Life Saver Fairy as much as we do.

This next thing has got to be the coolest Life Saver Fairy event in the world. One time our whole family went on a trip for a couple of days. When we got back, it was pretty late at night, and the Life Saver Fairy had paid us a visit at our house. It was so cool. Cole and I went up to our bedrooms and noticed a Life Saver on the floor in front of each of our bedroom doors.

Cole saw the one in front of his door first and yelled to me, "The Life Saver Fairy was here!"

We both went in our rooms, thinking we would have to look all over to see where she hid the Life Savers. But much to our surprise, the Life Savers weren't hidden. They were all over the place! There must have been a hundred of them scattered all over the floors and on top of our beds. There were some on top of the dressers, some on the window sills and more in the closet. She even put a couple in each of our drawers. We both ran downstairs screaming and hollering, "The Life Saver Fairy was here! You've got to come up and see this! It is sooo cool!"

My mom and dad weren't nearly as excited as we were, but they did finally come up and look. When they saw all the Life Savers, they had to admit it was pretty darn impressive.

Then Cole and I ran downstairs and went flying out the back door onto the deck and started yelling as loud as we could, "THANK YOU, LIFE SAVER FAIRY! THANK YOU, LIFE SAVER FAIRY! THANK YOU VERY, VERY MUCH! YOU'RE THE COOLEST LIFE SAVER FAIRY IN THE WHOLE WORLD!"

My dad came out and told us to get in the house. "Do you two realize what time it is? It's after midnight. One of the neighbors is probably calling the police right now for disturbing the peace. I've heard enough about the Life Saver Fairy for one night. Now get upstairs and get to bed."

When I finally went to bed, I got one more surprise. I crawled under the covers and was trying to get comfortable, but I kept feeling lumps under my sheet down by my feet.

I couldn't figure out what it could possibly be, and then all of a sudden it hit me. The Life Saver Fairy must have put some Life Savers under my sheet. When I pulled the Life Savers out from under the sheet, I knew what I had to do. I had to holler "thank you."

"THANKS AGAIN, LIFE SAVER FAIRY!" This time I didn't holler it very loud cuz I didn't want my dad to get any madder than he already was. He must have heard me anyway.

"If I hear one more word about the Life Saver Fairy, I'm going to introduce you to the Spanking Fairy. Do you understand?"

Anyway, as long as I live, I'm always going to believe in the Life Saver Fairy no matter what . . . or at least until she doesn't leave me anymore Life Savers.

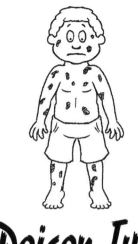

Poison Ivy

Every now and then, my brother and I can come up with some pretty stupid ideas of our own. Only when *we* come up with a stupid idea, it's not always that funny, and one of us usually gets in trouble or gets hurt or something else bad.

We went to one of my sister's softball games once. After about two innings, we got bored cuz my sister is only eight years old, and when eight-year-old girls play fast-pitch softball, nothing happens. Almost everybody on both teams either gets walked or strikes out. It definitely was the most boring game I had ever been to, and to make it worse, we couldn't just leave and go home cuz we came with our mom and dad. My brother and I started wandering around, looking for something else to do.

We walked to the other side of the outfield fence where there was this big hill, and at the bottom of the hill there were some soccer fields. We decided to go down the hill and watch one of the soccer games.

When we got about half-way down, my stupid brother said, "Let's roll down the rest of the way. Come on, I'll race ya!"

We had so much fun rolling down that hill that we decided to go all the way to the top and roll down again. We must have done it three or four times before we finally quit. How were we supposed to know there was more than just grass growing on that hill?

The next day my brother broke out with red blotches all over his body. He had the worst case of poison ivy you can imagine. My dad said it was worse than the time he got poison ivy working for the landscaping company. He had to go to the doctor, it was so bad.

At first, I was pretty worried. I figured if Cole got it from rolling down the hill, and I was rolling down the hill with him, I was sure to get it, too.

After two days went by, I hadn't gotten any red, blotchy spots at all, and Cole had them all over both of his legs and arms and even some on his belly. I was pretty sure I wouldn't catch it, so now I thought it was kind of funny. I'd laugh at him when he came out of the bathroom cuz he'd have this pink lotion all over his body and he'd say how much the poison ivy itched.

I guess I never should have laughed at him. It wasn't long before I came down with a couple of spots on my legs. At first they didn't itch, so I wasn't even sure it was poison ivy. But it wasn't very long before my worst nightmare came true. When I went to change my clothes for gym, the two little spots turned into one, huge, red, puffy blotch that was the size of a soccer ball and itched like crazy. I spent the rest of the afternoon trying to gently rub my leg without really scratching cuz I heard my dad tell Cole that, if he scratched the poison ivy, it would spread.

Well, my dad was wrong, cuz even though I wasn't scratching, the poison ivy was spreading. By the time I got home from school, I had it practically everywhere on my body. Now my poison ivy was a lot worse than Cole's. And what made it worse—Cole's poison ivy was starting to get better.

I couldn't believe how much this stuff itched. It felt like a thousand mosquitoes bit me at the same time or there were a million little ants crawling under my skin. I wanted to go out in the garage and get the wire brush my dad uses to clean the grill and start working it up and down my arms and legs. I didn't care if you weren't supposed to scratch it. I WANTED TO SCRATCH! The stupid pink stuff that my mom gave me to stop the itching just wasn't working.

The next day my grandpa came over to see how I was doing. "So how bad is the poison ivy?" he asked.

I was in my boxer shorts, so I stood up and said, "See for yourself. It's on both of my legs, my back, my stomach and my arms, and it's even in my armpits."

Grandpa sort of chuckled, then checked it out and told me it looked pretty bad. "Well, I have to admit, you look pretty cute with that pink stuff all over you."

"Ha, ha, Grandpa. Very funny. This stuff really itches."

"I know how bad it itches, Luke. I had poison ivy once myself. And, it was definitely worse than your poison ivy and Cole's put together."

"Oh sure, Grandpa!"

"I'm serious," he said. "It started out like yours on my legs and arms, and then it spread to my belly and my back. Before I knew it, the stuff had spread to my neck and armpits. I even got a couple of spots on my face and ears. I was just beginning to think it had stopped spreading and I was finally getting better when it spread to the worst place it could possibly spread . . ."

Grandpa didn't say anything for a minute, and at first I didn't know what he was talking about. But then I realized what he meant.

"You mean the poison ivy even spread to your, you know . . . down there?"

"Yup, it even spread down there. And, unfortunately, it was in both places . . . down there. Talk about embarrassing. It wasn't like I could scratch *down there* every time it itched either."

I started laughing. I tried not to, but I couldn't help it.

"It wasn't funny!" my grandpa said. He tried to act serious, but when I looked over at him, I could see that he was laughing, too. Then my grandpa said, "You better quit laughing. It still could happen to you!"

That night, my grandpa came up with another one of his bright ideas. He called and told me he knew of a good cure for poison ivy. He said if you spread ice cream all over the poison ivy it not only helps stop the itching, but it also makes it go away quicker.

"Does it really?" I asked.

"Of course not, silly, but you tell your mom and dad that I told you I was coming over to spread ice cream on your poison ivy. Then I'll bring over the ice cream, and you and I will go upstairs to your bedroom and we'll eat the ice cream instead. We get all the ice cream and nobody else gets any."

Grandpa came over with the ice cream just like he said, and we went up to my room and ate it. Nobody bothered us, even though my mom and dad knew we were eating the ice cream, not spreading it on the poison ivy. Then when Grandpa and I were almost finished, Grandpa said, "Let's spread the rest of this all over your stomach and legs just to see what your mom and dad say."

When I came downstairs with ice cream smeared all over my body, my mom and dad hollered at me and told me to get upstairs and shower. They tried to find Grandpa so they could holler at him, too, but he had already left.

Little Sisters

The other day my grandpa came over to help my dad do something on our back porch. My dad was putting in a new light fixture, and my mom wanted Grandpa to make sure my dad didn't electrocute himself.

My grandpa always tries to do something funny when he's with my dad. When my dad was on the ladder, trying to take out the old fixture, my grandpa put his finger in Dad's side and went, "Zzzzzzzp!" My dad thought he was getting a shock, and he jumped back and almost fell off the ladder. It seemed pretty funny at the time, but I guess my dad could have been hurt if he had fallen off the ladder. Sometimes my grandpa doesn't think before he does something funny. And not everybody thinks it's funny.

After Grandpa finished working with my dad, he came up to my room and asked me how my book was coming along. I told him it had been going pretty good, but now I was stuck.

"I must have writer's stump or something like that." I said.

"Writer's stump? What's that?" Grandpa asked.

"You know, when you can't think of the next thing you want to say, so you're stumped and don't know what to write next. My teacher told us about it when we were doing a writing assignment for school."

Grandpa rubbed his chin and thought for a few seconds, then said, "Oh, you mean writer's block, not writer's stump. I've heard of that. So, what's got you stumped?"

"Well, most of my stories are about Cole and me and you. And I wanted to write something about my sister. But, most of the time Tate is a pain in the you-know-what, so I'm not sure what to do. Were your sisters a pain when you were my age, Grandpa?"

"I had three sisters, but only one of them, Mary, was around my age. She was the only one that ever bugged me. My brother David and I were real close, and we did everything together. We didn't like it when she came around and tried to interfere with what we were doing. David would always try to get her to leave by doing something gross."

"What would your brother do to gross her out?"

Grandpa said, "One time David and I were playing in the back yard, and Mary came out and sat down right where we were trying to play. She pretended she was playing, but all she was really doing was drawing pictures in the dirt.

We told her to leave, but she said she didn't have to.

"David was chewing on a piece of gum, and when Mary wasn't looking he took it out of his mouth, dropped it on the ground, and stepped on it. Then he kicked it over next to her and said, 'Hey Mary, I found this piece of gum on the ground, do you want it?'

"She just looked at him and said, 'That's gross.'

"David said, 'I don't know; it looks pretty good to me,' and he picked it up and put it in his mouth then started chewing it right in front of her.

"Mary looked at David and said, 'I know that was your gum cuz I saw you chewing it when I came out here,' and she never left.

"The next time he tried to gross her out, though, it worked. That time was really gross."

I wasn't sure I wanted to hear a story that was grosser than chewing dirty, old gum, but Grandpa told me anyway.

"We were playing in a vacant lot that we called the Mountains. I guess we called it the Mountains cuz there was a big hill in the back of the lot, and calling it the Mountains made the hill seem bigger than it actually was. We had this really cool fort that we had built in back of some bushes, and it was camouflaged so you could hardly see it.

"Anyway, we were catching grasshoppers. We had caught about ten of them and put them in a jar when, all of a sudden, Mary came from out of nowhere and wanted to know what we were doing. We didn't want her snooping around where she might find our fort, so we showed her the jar of grasshoppers. There were streaks of brown grasshopper spit all over the inside of the jar. She looked at the jar and said, 'Gross.' Then she told us we should let them go, cuz if we didn't, the grasshoppers were going to die.

"David didn't want her hanging around anymore, telling us what to do, so he took one of the grasshoppers out of the jar and waited until it spit tobacco juice on his hand. We always called the brown stuff tobacco juice, but we knew it was just grasshopper spit. Then he took his hand and put it real close to Mary's face, like he was going to smear the tobacco juice on her face. She didn't even move. She just said, 'Go ahead and put that nasty, old juice on me. I'll just go home and show Mom what you did.' So, instead of putting it on her face, he takes his hand and starts licking the tobacco juice off right in front of her. When he finished licking that hand, he started in on the other hand and asked her if she wanted a taste. Finally, Mary said, 'You're an idiot,' and left."

"Your brother actually ate grasshopper spit?" I said.

"Yup, but he paid the price for it."

"What do you mean? You said your sister left, and that's what you wanted, wasn't it?"

"Well, yes, we did want her to leave, so that part was good. But after awhile David started to get a stomach ache, so we had to go home. When we got home, Mary and my mom were sitting on the front porch. They could tell David was sick just by looking at him.

"My mom asked David what was wrong, and he said his stomach hurt. Then she asked him what he had eaten, but before he could answer he said, 'I have to go throw up,' and went to the bathroom. My mom looked at me and asked if I knew whether he ate anything that would make him sick. I just shrugged my shoulders. I looked at my sister, and she had a smile on her face that made me think she was ready to spill the beans about the grasshopper spit. I was pretty sure David was in trouble now.

"My sister looked at my mom and said, 'Maybe he ate something bad at breakfast or he swallowed his gum. That could make him sick.'

"I couldn't believe it. Here was my sister's chance to get David in trouble and she didn't. She could have said she saw him eat grasshopper spit, but instead she actually helped him out.

"After that, I had a different respect for my sister, and we started to become pretty good friends. She was still a pain in the butt once in awhile, but then maybe she thought I was a pain in her butt, too. It didn't matter. She turned out to be a really cool sister. Just think about that when you write about Tate."

"So, did your mom ever find out that your brother ate grasshopper spit?" I asked.

"I don't think so," he said. "But she made him take two big spoonfuls of cod liver oil, and that stuff is really nasty tasting. You can bet he never ate grasshopper spit again."

So, like I said before, I have a little sister, Tate. Sometimes she can be a pain in the butt, like when I'm trying to play hockey on my new Play Station and she asks me a bunch of questions, or she bugs me when I'm using the bathroom. Sometimes, when I'm trying to watch TV, she keeps dancing in front of me with her stupid pom-poms, pretending she's a cheerleader and blocking the TV. One time when she was practicing her cheerleading moves, she asked me to be the other cheerleader. I told her no at first, but she kept bugging me, so I finally did.

She gave me two little pillows to use as pom-poms and kept saying, "You're supposed to swing your arms in a circle to the left, not the right."

When we faced each other and were supposed to put our pom-poms together, I hit her in the face with the pillows instead. The next thing you know, we were on the floor, wrestling. Our mom had to holler at us to break it up.

Most of the time Tate is pretty cool, and we get along okay. I suppose one of the reasons I think she's pretty cool is cuz she's from Russia. We adopted her when she was seven years old. When she came to live with us, she couldn't speak a word of English, but now that she has lived here for two years, we can't get her to shut up. That's probably one of the reasons I think she's a pain.

One of the best reasons about having a sister who's only a couple of years younger than me is, when I can't play with Cole, I can play with her. Usually, I just have her stand in front of my hockey net down in the basement and I take shots at her with my plastic puck. I keep telling her she's a really good goalie, but the truth is, she kinda sucks at it.

I told her she was a really good goalie cuz I wanted her to keep playing with me in the basement. But, believe me, that was a big mistake. She signed up for hockey tryouts and said she wanted to be a goalie. I tried to explain to my dad that he shouldn't let her try out cuz she wasn't really any good. He just said I was jealous cuz now I might have a sister that plays hockey.

Actually, I was afraid she might end up on my team. Even though she is two years younger than me, her birthday is in the middle of the hockey season, so she could be placed in my age group. How embarrassing would that be, having your little sister on your hockey team? And what's worse—having her be the goalie!

Well, it turned out they put her in the age group below me that was an all-girls' team, so I didn't have that to worry. But having a sister that plays hockey does have some problems. Since we can't ever get her to shut up, all I hear is, "Guess how many saves I got today," or "They let me play center and I scored a goal today." Stuff like that.

One time my sister's breezers got put in my hockey bag by mistake, and I didn't find out until I went to put them on at practice. Normally, that wouldn't have been a problem cuz we wear the same size breezers and they're both black. But, since my sister's team is all girls, they decided to put a small, white, frilly piece of cloth around the top of their breezers. I didn't notice it until I put the breezers on and everybody on my team saw it. They almost laughed me out of the locker room. I had to tear it off cuz I didn't have any other breezers to wear, and I sure wasn't going to skate with that on.

When I got home, I was mad at Tate for putting her breezers in my bag, and Tate was mad at me for tearing off her stupid cloth, and my mom was mad at both of us. Sisters sure can be a pain sometimes.

Wiffle Ball

In the summertime, my brother and I play a lot of baseball in either our backyard or in one of our friends' backyards. We play it with a regular bat and a tennis ball. Most of the time, we have a lot of fun, but sometimes my brother and I fight. And when we do, the game is pretty much over cuz one of us usually ends up hurt. Most of the time, it's me.

It's pretty cool, though, cuz a regular baseball bat can hit a tennis ball about a mile if you hit it just right . . . okay, not a mile, but it can hit it over the house in back of ours if you connect just right. My brother can hit it further than me cuz he's bigger than me. He also plays baseball all summer long, while I play soccer, so he *should* be able to hit better than me.

This one time I was getting mad at my brother cuz he wouldn't give me any good pitches to hit. He kept trying to pitch them real fast so I couldn't hit them, but I wouldn't swing at them, and we have a rule saying you can only strike out if you swing at the ball.

"Come on, Luke, you gotta swing at something," my brother said.

"You're pitching them too fast. I'm not gonna swing 'til you throw me a good one."

We kept arguing back and forth for about ten minutes, and all the other kids were starting to get mad at us. I was pretty sure it wouldn't be long until everybody left and the game would be over. Finally, I decided that I didn't care anymore if I got a hit or not, so when Cole threw the next pitch, I closed my eyes and swung the bat as hard as I could.

SMACK! Somehow I managed to hit the ball perfect, and when it came flying off the bat, it went straight at Cole.

"Ooooph!" he screamed when the ball hit him, and he fell right to the ground. I thought the ball hit him in the stomach and knocked the wind out of him, but when I heard him moaning and saw where he was holding his hands, I knew the ball hit him in the . . . you know . . . down there.

I ran out to see if he was okay, and so did the others. We watched him roll around on the ground with his knees tucked all the way up to his chin moaning, "Oooh! Oooh!"

"Where'd you get hit?" one of the kids asked, laughing.

We didn't need an answer cuz we all knew exactly where he got hit: right square in the gonads.

He wasn't crying, or at least I didn't think he was crying, but he kept moaning and rolling on the ground. We all laughed at first until we realized that he really was hurt. Then we kind of felt bad for laughing. He did look pretty funny, though, rolling around on the ground—holding himself.

When Cole was finally able to go into the house, I told my mom what happened. She was pretty concerned cuz Cole just plopped down on the couch, still holding his privates and still moaning.

Finally, my mom told me to go back outside and play so she could check out Cole and find out how bad he really was. I told her I wanted to stay, but she said she didn't need me there, laughing and bugging him. Then she told Cole to go downstairs to his bedroom, and she would find out if he needed to go to the doctor.

I went outside and snuck around the side of the house where Cole's bedroom window was. The shades were pulled tight so I couldn't see into the room, but his window was open, and I could hear the two of them talking.

"It doesn't look like I need to take you to the doctor, but it does look a little swollen. You need to put an ice pack on it and rest for awhile."

When I heard the part about the ice pack, I started laughing, and my mom must have heard me. "Luke, you better get away from that window before I make it so you need an ice pack on your rear-end. Do you hear me?"

Cole must have been hurt pretty bad, cuz that night when he came up for supper he was still holding the ice pack on his privates. But at least he wasn't moaning anymore.

A couple of days later, I told my grandpa what happened and asked him if he ever got hit in his privates with a tennis ball when he was my age. He said that he and his brother never did play backyard baseball with a tennis ball when they were little, but they used to play Wiffle ball all the time.

When I asked him what Wiffle ball was, he said, "Wiffle ball is a little like your backyard baseball, only it's played with a plastic bat and a plastic ball. The plastic ball has a bunch of holes in it, so no matter how hard you hit the ball, it can't go very far and won't break any windows. Oh yeah, and it never did hurt if you got hit in the privates."

"So how did you play it?" I asked.

"Well, we didn't have big backyards and lots of open space, like you have here. All the yards were really small, and they all had some kind of fence around them, so everybody had to pretty much play in their own yard. And the backyards didn't have much grass, which meant we were always playing in the dirt and rocks.

"My brother, David, and I were pretty good at making up games, so we made up Wiffle Ball Baseball. Just like in your game, one person pitched while the other person batted. The batter stood way back by the fence, facing the back of the house. He had to try and hit the ball against the back of the house. Where the ball would hit on the house determined whether the batter got a single, double, triple or homerun. The higher you hit the ball on the house, the more bases you got. Once the batter hit the ball, the pitcher had to run up to the house and try and catch the ball before it hit the ground.

If he caught the ball, it was an out. David and I could play that stupid game for hours and never get tired of it.

"We used to get up at about six-thirty in the morning during the summer and wait until our dad went to work and our mom went back to bed, then we would sneak out in the backyard and start playing."

"Six-thirty in the morning," I said. "Why so early?"

"Because that way our brothers and sisters wouldn't bother us. If they came out and wanted to play and we wouldn't let them, they would tell our mom, and then she would say nobody could play. We tried to tell her that only two people could play the game at a time. She wouldn't listen. She would always say 'Well then, make up a new game where everybody can play, because if everybody can't play, then nobody can play. That's my rule.'

"Another thing that ended our game was when one of us hit the ball into Mrs. Sima's yard. Mrs. Sima was our next door neighbor."

"Why didn't you just go get it back?" I asked.

"It wasn't like we could just hop over the fence and pick up our ball. You see, Mrs. Sima was one of the meanest, grumpiest old ladies in the whole world. She lived all by herself, and she was kind of hunched over because she was so old, and she had a big old purple-and-black wart on her forehead that almost covered one of her eyes. She was scary looking. And she didn't want anybody in her precious yard. She had told us more than once that, if we hit the ball in her yard, we'd be sorry.

"Well, this one time David hit a foul ball into her yard right after we started playing. The ball landed behind a big bushy plant, so there was no way Mrs. Sima could see it from inside her house. David and I went back in the alley and stood by the bushes, trying to figure out how we could get the ball before she came out and caught us.

"I tried to coax my brother into getting the ball. 'Come on, David,' I said. 'Jump over the fence and get the ball. Even if she does come out, she'll never get you before you get the ball.' David argued that I should go get it because he went and got it the last time. I said, 'Yeah, but you hit it in her yard the last time, and you know the rule: whoever hits the ball in her yard has to go get it. Now go get it before she comes out to work in her yard and finds it.' My brother finally got up enough nerve to jump over the fence and try to retrieve the ball before the old lady came out.

"I watched as David stayed crouched down real low behind a bush for a few seconds, waiting to see if the old lady was coming. When she didn't come out, I hollered, 'Hurry up and get the ball so we can play.' The ball was almost in the middle of the yard, so David had to go about thirty feet before he could grab it, throw it over the fence into our yard, and then get the heck out of there before the old lady caught him. Finally, David took off and ran toward the ball. The old lady must have been watching us the whole time, because as soon as David got near the ball, the back door came flying open, and she was headed down the porch steps after David.

"The old lady hollered, 'I told you kids to stay out of my yard. What do you think you're doing? Now get out of here! Do you hear me?'

"I started yelling, 'RUN, DAVID, RUN! GET OUT OF THERE!'

"I thought David would just turn around, run back to the fence and jump back over, but he didn't. David kept going until he got to the ball. He reached down and grabbed it and threw it over into our yard, then headed to the corner of her yard where he hoped he could climb over the fence before the old lady caught him. I watched as the old lady chased after David. She was pretty fast for an old lady, but not as fast as David. David went to the corner of her yard, knowing it would be easier to get over the fence there. He climbed to the top of the fence and threw one leg over. Then, just as David started to throw his other leg over, I heard the old lady scream, 'If I catch you, I'll wring your neck! Do hear me?'

"She reached the fence just as David pushed off, and that's when I heard a loud ripping noise. When David hit the ground and started running down the alley, all you could see was his underwear, because the whole backside of his shorts was torn off and still hanging on the fence. Then the old lady turned and looked right at the bush where I was hiding and said, 'That'll teach you, ya little brats.'

"The funny thing about the old lady was she never did tell our mom. I think she just wanted us to come in her yard so she could chase us and scare the heck out of us. I'm not sure what she would have done if she ever caught us. I just know she was definitely the meanest, ugliest old lady I ever met."

I asked my grandpa if that story was really true, and he said, "Every word of it. If you don't I believe me, ask your great-uncle David. And if you don't believe him, go back to Mrs. Sima's yard and see the piece of David's shorts still hanging on the fence for yourself."

A couple of days later, I told my dad what Grandpa had said and asked him if we could go to Grandpa's old house and see if Great-uncle David's pants were still hanging on the fence.

My dad just shook his head and said, "Don't be such a knucklehead. That happened over fifty years ago . . . if it even happened at all."

I asked my grandpa for Great-uncle David's phone number. I figured there was only one way to find out the truth and that was to call David and ask him myself. David said it was true except for the part about who hit the ball in the yard. He said Grandpa hit the ball in her yard but was too scared to get it, so he had to. I'm not sure who was telling the truth, but I think I'm going to believe Grandpa. After all, he is my grandpa.

The Bucket Story

The last time I talked about my book with my grandpa, he told me I should tell some stories about myself once in a while, instead of only stories about him. He said that would make the book more interesting. So, before I tell you one of my grandpa's ice fishing stories, I'll tell you a fish story that happened to me last night.

I guess it's not exactly a fish story, but it sort of is. When I woke up this morning, my bed was soaking wet. It was wet all over my sheet and blanket, but I knew I didn't wet the bed cuz my boxer shorts were dry. (Now that I'm in middle school, I sleep in boxer shorts instead of pajamas.)

It didn't take me long to figure out what happened, especially when I saw Biggie lying next to my pillow. In case you didn't know, Biggie is my pet goldfish. Well, he used to be my pet goldfish. Now he's just my dead goldfish. I called him Biggie cuz he had big lips.

I woke up last night cuz there was a thunderstorm. I don't like thunderstorms, and they almost always wake me up. As I was listening to the crashes of thunder, I remembered that Biggie always gets scared during a thunderstorm, too. I can tell he's scared cuz instead of swimming in circles like he always does, Biggie goes back and forth real fast. Sometimes he goes so fast he bumps his lips on the inside of the fish bowl. That's probably how his lips got so big.

Anyway, I got up and brought Biggie and his fish bowl to bed with me and tried to calm him down by singing to him. Usually that will settle him right down. I know that seems dumb, singing to a goldfish; but if I sing "I'm Forever Blowing Bubbles" enough times, Biggie will actually blow some bubbles. Last night, no matter how many times I sang the song, Biggie just wouldn't settle down.

Well, the thunderstorm must have lasted longer than I figured, and I must have fallen asleep; and when I fell asleep, the fish bowl must have tipped over; and when the fish bowl tipped over, Biggie must have flopped all the way up to my pillow before he finally croaked. He was probably trying to flop himself onto my face to wake me up, but he never made it. Poor Biggie.

But worst of all, when my mom found out what happened, she hollered at me big time cuz she had to change my sheets. It's a good thing Biggie's fish bowl didn't break when it fell on the floor, or I probably would have been grounded.

Now I've got to decide whether to flush Biggie down the

toilet, like most people would do with their dead goldfish, or bury him out in the backyard somewhere. I think I'll go bury him in the backyard cuz what if Biggie came back to life while he was down in the sewer swimming around with all that . . . you know . . . poop and stuff? That would be just too disgusting!

So that's my fish story.

My grandpa's fish story is more gross. One day my dad and Cole went ice fishing and came home after catching about fifteen sunfish.

When my grandpa came over to see the fish, my dad said, "We would have caught more, but we had to come home so Cole could go to the bathroom."

My grandpa looked over at Cole and asked, "Why didn't you just go behind the car?"

Cole turned a little red in the face and said, "Because, Grandpa, I had to go number two, that's why. I couldn't very well do that out on the lake in the middle of the day, could I?"

My grandpa started laughing and told Cole he was just like his dad. He said our dad had that same problem once when he was ice fishing, only the outcome was worse. Since my dad had already gone in the house, Cole and I asked Grandpa what my dad did that was worse. Grandpa sat down on the step and told us.

"Your dad was about eight years old at the time, and I took him ice fishing with my brother, David. We were all the way up north at Mille Lacs Lake, and we had rented a fish house. You wouldn't believe the size of this lake. It was so big that we had to drive almost a half hour on the lake just to get to the fish house. Fifteen minutes after we got to the fish house and started fishing, your dad came over to me and said, 'I have to go potty.'

"I told him, 'Well, when you're ice fishing and you have to go potty, you go outside next to the fish house; that's where you go potty.' Your dad kind of hung his head for a couple of minutes then finally went outside to do his business. He was gone for a long time, and I was just about ready to go out and see what had happened to him when he finally came back in. He stood there hanging his head, and I knew that something was bothering him so I asked him what was wrong. Your dad whispered in my ear, 'I have to go number two.'"

When Cole and I started laughing, my grandpa held up his hand and said, "Wait a minute, that's not the funniest part. Let me finish." We stopped laughing so Grandpa could finish telling the story. We always liked it when Grandpa told embarrassing stuff about our dad.

"Anyway, your dad tells me he has to go number two and he has to go *really* bad. I handed your dad the fish bucket and told him if he has to go number two then he should go outside and do his business in the bucket because there aren't any bathrooms in this fish house. Your dad picked up the fish bucket and headed back outside to do his business.

"After about ten minutes, the fish house door opened up and your dad came back in with an empty bucket and that same, sad look on his face. He said, 'I can't do it outside, it's too cold. Can I just go in the bucket in here?' Well, your great-uncle David looked at me and said, 'Oh, let the poor kid go potty in here.' So I did."

Cole stood up and said, "Oh my gosh, Grandpa! Are you telling me my dad pooped in the fish bucket right there in the fish house? Did it stink?"

"Did it *stink*? Are you kidding? By the time your dad got done pooping in that bucket, the fish house stunk bad enough that we had to leave the door open so long our fish holes were starting to freeze over. David couldn't pull up one of the fish he caught because he needed one hand to keep his nose plugged."

Me and Cole started laughing so hard we fell off the steps into the snow. We kept laughing and yelling, "My dad went poop in the fish bucket!"

"Finally, your dad took the bucket outside. He was supposed to clean it out, but he didn't and the poop froze to the bottom of the bucket. When we were all done fishing, I told your dad to go outside and put all the fish in the fish bucket. He came back in with the fish bucket and said he forgot to get rid of the poop and now it was stuck to the bottom of the bucket. We ended up leaving the fish there because there was no way we were going to put them in the same bucket that your dad pooped in."

When my dad came out to find out what all the fuss was about, both Cole and I pointed at him and chanted, "You pooped in the fish bucket! You pooped in the fish bucket!"

My dad looked at Grandpa and said, "Did you tell them the story about when we went fishing at Mille Lacs Lake?" Before Grandpa could answer, my dad said, "Well be sure and tell them who caught the most fish that day. It was me! I caught the most fish that day, even if I did have to you-know-what in the fish bucket."

Grandpa said, "That's right, you did. But the fish never made it home because we weren't about to put them in your poop bucket."

A Trick on Dad

My grandpa picked me up from school today. On the way home, he asked me if I had finished my book. I told him I was only halfway through with it. I told him that I took his advice and wrote some things about myself besides all the stories about him. Then I asked him if he remembered any more stories about when he was a kid.

"Well," Grandpa said, "David and I did like to goof around a lot, so I'm sure I can tell you other stories about when I was a kid."

"What kind of stuff did you do?"

"We messed around quite a bit when we went ice fishing with our dad. Most of the time, it was just stupid stuff, like saying something to try and get the other person mad or pretending to accidentally drop someone's hat in the fish hole but really doing it on purpose. You know, dumb stuff like that. If we got too loud and wild, our dad would finally say, 'All right you two, if that's all you're going to do is bicker and fight, then you can go outside and sit in the cold car and fight out there. That way I won't have to listen to you . . . and it's pretty D#%=@* cold in that car.' [That's how you write a bad word without actually writing it. I learned that from my grandpa.] Anyway, he never did make us go out in the car, but he sure did threaten us a lot."

"Did you ever play any tricks on your dad? Cole and I do with our dad, but sometimes he gets pretty mad."

"Once in awhile we tried to, but he was usually too smart for us, so the trick hardly ever worked—except for this one time. I'll never forget the one trick we played on him that really got him good."

"Did you put his hat in the fish hole like you did to your brother? I'll bet that would have made him pretty mad."

"No way! We may not have been very smart, but we weren't that stupid. We knew better than to do something that would get us in trouble. Our trick was really cool, but before I can tell you what we did, I'll have to explain how we fished for walleyes. When you're ice fishing for walleyes, you can't just jerk on the line as soon as your bobber goes down, like you do for other fish. You have to let the walleye take your bobber for a long time, and then when your line stops, that's when you jerk on the line and pull him in.

"Anyway, our dad usually fell asleep a couple of hours after we started fishing. That's when me and my brother would start goofing around, and that's when we pulled a good one on our dad. When he fell asleep, David and I decided to tie something heavy on our dad's fishing line and drop it in his hole, so when his bobber went down, he would think he had a fish. We first tried a banana. It felt heavy enough so we tied one on his line and put it in his hole. What we didn't realize was that bananas float, so it didn't work."

"Didn't your dad wake up and catch you?" I asked

"When our dad fell asleep fishing, he was out like a light. About the only thing that would wake him up was the sound of his fishing reel turning when a fish was taking his bait.

"Anyway, we needed something that wouldn't float, so we decided to use one of our dad's cans of beer. The beer can worked perfect for two reasons: first, it was easy to put the hook through the pull tab on the top of the can; and, second, it turned out to be just the right weight so, when we put it in the water, it dropped slowly to the bottom of the lake.

"When our dad's bobber went down, his fishing reel started to turn and that turning noise woke him up. Me and David were both sitting on our chairs, looking at our fish holes when he woke up. He looked at his bobber and saw it was completely out of sight and said, 'Well, it looks like I'm the only one who's going to catch any fish around here.' David and I did everything we could to keep from laughing as we watched him pull up his line. When the beer can finally came to the top of the hole, and our dad could see what it was, he stopped pulling and said, 'Well aren't you two boys cute. I'll bet you think that's pretty funny, don't you?' Both of us fell out of our chairs laughing as our dad held up his prize fish, a can of beer on the end of his fishing line."

"I can't believe your dad didn't get mad at you," I said. "Didn't he do anything to you?"

"No, he just shook his finger at us and said, 'Someday, I'm going to get the two of you back for this and don't you forget it.' That's all he said."

Mean Tricks

I pulled a mean trick on my brother the other day. He was taking a shower and didn't lock the bathroom door; so I opened the door, reached in and turned out the light. Then I closed the door and raced outside to my friend's house. I could hear my brother screaming all the way down the block.

I thought it was funny at the time; but when I got home, I found out that, when he tried to turn the light back on, my brother bruised his leg on a drawer he had left open. When my mom found out, she was mad as heck. She made me stay in the house that night, so maybe it wasn't very funny.

A couple of days later, I told my grandpa what I did and asked him if he ever played any tricks on his brothers.

"David and I were always playing some kind of trick on each other," he said.

"So did you ever get in trouble like I did?"

"Once in a while, but most of the time our mom and dad never found out."

"Can you think of any that I can write in my book?" I asked.

"Well, this one time David and I were washing up, and I was all done and my brother was still in the shower. I was ready to leave and saw my brother's underwear sitting on the floor and said, 'Hey, David, do you need your underwear?' David said, 'What do you mean do I need my underwear? Of course, I do.' So I said, 'Okay, here ya go,' and I threw David's underwear in the shower with him so it got all wet. When my brother started screaming, I just said, 'Hey, you said you needed your underwear.' "

"That's a pretty good one, Grandpa! I can't wait to try that on Cole someday. Can you think of any more?"

"Let me think. When your dad was about your age, he and I used to try to play an April Fool's Day trick on each other every year. Maybe you can write about that."

"My dad did? Really? Did he ever pull a good one on you?"

"I have to admit; one year he got me pretty good. This happened when your dad was in middle school. I was always the first one to get up in the morning because I had to leave for work before your dad and his brother went to school. I would always get dressed, then go in the kitchen and make my coffee. Back then, I had to wear a shirt and tie to work.

"On this particular April Fool's Day, when I started to fill the coffee pot with water, the water didn't come out of the faucet like it was supposed to. It came out of the sink sprayer instead and sprayed all over my clean shirt and tie. Someone had cleverly taped down the sprayer handle and pointed it right at the place where I would be standing.

"I screamed and hollered, but neither your dad nor your uncle would admit to doing it. They both just stayed in their bedrooms yelling, 'April Fools!' Later that day, I found out it was your dad who did it, but by that time, I wasn't mad any more. I just told him I would get even someday."

"Did you have to change your shirt and tie?" I asked.

"Of course, I did. The water came out so fast and hard it was like standing in the shower with my clothes on. And then I had to clean up the floor, too. He definitely pulled a good one on me that year."

"So did you get him back, Grandpa?"

"Yup, the next year I got even. At least I thought so anyway."

"I don't know, Grandpa, that seemed like a pretty good trick. What did you do that was better than that one?"

"Your dad was always the next person to get up and use the bathroom after I left for work, so I set up a little surprise for him. When your dad sat down on the toilet to do his morning business, his rear end stuck to the toilet seat. My little surprise was a thin coating of clear molasses on the toilet. Molasses is a real thick, sticky kind of syrup."

I started laughing. "My dad got his butt stuck to the toilet seat? That had to be pretty funny."

"Your dad thought it was glue and that his butt was permanently stuck to the toilet seat! He tried to tell his mom that he couldn't go to school because his butt was glued to the toilet seat. When she said she would come in and help him get it *unstuck*, he decided that would be too embarrassing, so he took care of it himself. It wasn't easy, though. Your dad tried to wipe off the molasses with toilet paper, but the toilet paper kept sticking to his rear end. Believe me; it turned out to be a real mess! He ended up having to take a shower in order to get all the toilet paper and molasses off his butt and almost missed his bus."

That was so funny! I couldn't wait to tell my brother about it. I asked Grandpa if he remembered any more tricks I could write about.

"Well, my brother David did a pretty mean trick to your dad one time. I think you can write about this one."

"Oh good, another one about my dad," I said.

"We'll call this the Dandelion Trick. David did it to your dad when your dad was only three or four years old.

"This is what happened. There was a family picnic on Memorial Day, and David was showing all the little kids how to pick the fluffy dandelions and blow the seeds at each other. He told one of the kids, 'Watch this!' And when they did, he would blow the dandelion seeds all over them. The kids thought it was pretty funny.

"Finally, David asked them if they wanted to see a really

cool trick. Your dad kept yelling 'I do, I do!' So David called him up to the middle of the group and explained what he was going to do. David took a big, fluffy dandelion and broke off a small piece of the stem and gave it to your dad and told him to hide it anywhere he wanted to. David said, 'You can put it in your pocket, under your hat, in your shoe, in your shirt or anywhere you want, and I'll be able to find it just by moving the fluffy dandelion all around your body.' David told him to go ahead and hide it, that he wouldn't look.

"So your dad hid the little piece of stem somewhere on his body. David took the rest of the dandelion with the big fluffy head full of dandelion seeds and started moving it all around your dad's body.

"After a long time of waving the dandelion all over your dad's body, David finally held it near your dad's lips and said, 'It's in your mouth!' When your dad shook his head and told David it wasn't, David said, 'I know it's in there! Open your mouth so I can see.' Your dad opened his mouth, and that's when David did one of the meanest things I've ever seen; he shoved the dandelion head in your dad's mouth, and all those seeds stuck to his tongue and the inside of his cheeks. Your dad started coughing and spitting, trying to get the dandelion seeds out. He even tried to wipe off his tongue with his shirt sleeve."

"Did he cry?" I asked.

"Nope, he never did cry, but he kept spitting out dandelion seeds for the rest of the afternoon."

"That was pretty mean. But I'll bet you and your brother did meaner tricks than that to each other." I said.

"David and I did mess with each other and many times that goofing around ended up with one of us doing something mean. In fact, I remember two things that I did to my brother that I thought were going to be funny but they ended up not being funny at all."

"Why? Did one of you get hurt or something?"

"Just let me finish," Grandpa said. "David and I liked to help out our dad with projects around the house, mainly because our dad always did those projects on Saturday, and Saturday was cleaning day, which meant we would get out of cleaning the rest of the house if we helped with our dad's project. Of course, that made our brothers and sisters mad as heck because then they'd have to do all the cleaning. But our dad would always tell them, 'Don't worry, I've got plenty for David and Jerry to do.'"

"So how come you wanted to help out your dad if he made you work? That doesn't sound like a very good deal. It seems like work is work."

"Just hang on," Grandpa said, "I'm getting to that. Okay, let's see . . . . Oh yeah, my brother and I knew that we would get to goof around more by helping our dad. And we also knew that, at some point, our dad would have to go to the hardware store for one thing or another. Whenever he went to the hardware store, he would always stop at the corner bar and have a beer with his buddies, and that meant we would get to have a glass of pop while our dad had his beer.

"Anyway, here's the first not-so-funny mean trick. Every spring, we had to take off the storm windows and put on the screens; and every fall, take off the screens and put on the storm windows. That was because we lived in a big old house that was built a couple of hundred years ago, and we didn't have the kind of windows like we do now. The windows were big and heavy, and some of them were so big that it took the two of us to carry one window.

"We were too small to carry a window up the ladder; so when our dad climbed up, we stayed down below on the ground and held the ladder so it wouldn't tip over. We would also go get stuff for our dad like a hammer or a screwdriver or a nail. When we did, we would always fight about who got to climb up the ladder and give it to him. Both of us loved to climb up the ladder so it wasn't easy trying to figure out who got to do it. Sometimes our dad would holler at us and tell us neither one of us could come up the ladder if we didn't quit fighting.

"Anyway, when we were standing around just holding the ladder, that's when the goofing around would begin, and that's when we usually got in trouble. I remember this one time, David picked a booger out of his nose and put it real close to my chin like he was going to put it on me, but he didn't because he knew he'd get in trouble if he did. So I decided I'd show him a thing or two and pulled out an even bigger booger from my nose and put it real close to his cheek the same way. David closed his eyes and said, 'I know you won't put it on me or you'll get in trouble.' Since David had his eyes closed, I lifted up one of my other fingers that didn't have a booger on it and wiped it on David's cheek. David thought it was the one with the booger on it, so he jumped backward screaming and bumped into the side of the ladder.

"There was a hammer hanging on one of the ladder rungs at the top of the ladder where our dad was working, and when David bumped the ladder, the hammer fell down and hit David right on the head. The hammer knocked David out cold. I got scared and hollered to my dad because David fell straight to the ground and didn't move. It seemed like it took forever for my dad to come down the ladder. The whole time he was coming down I wondered if my brother was dead, since I couldn't see him breathing.

"The look on my dad's face made me even more scared. He seemed worried, and I'd never seen my dad look worried before. He lifted up my brother's head and slapped him in the face a few times, and finally David started to moan.

"After I realized that David wasn't dead and he looked like he was going to be okay, I thought it was funny that he got slapped in the face, so I started to laugh. But my dad turned and looked at me with this cold, hard stare that told me it wasn't funny at all. 'Your brother could have been seriously hurt!' he said. 'This never would have happened if you two weren't goofing around.'

"David sat there, not even knowing what had happened. He was pretty mad at me for pretending to put a booger on him, and I was mad at him for making our dad come down the ladder and holler at me, and our dad was mad at both of us for goofing around."

"Did you get in trouble?" I asked. I'm pretty sure if this had happened to me and my brother, we would have been in trouble for sure.

"No, not really. When my dad realized that David was going to be all right, he told us we better not say anything to our mom about it. I think he told us that so *he* wouldn't get in trouble."

"Did you still get to help him on Saturdays after that or did you have to start cleaning the house with your brothers and sisters?"

"For a couple of weeks, he wouldn't let us help him. Then he decided to paint the house, and we were right back at it, goofing around. That's when the second thing happened.

"We were still too little to go up the ladder and paint— we wanted to do that more than anything—but at least Dad let us paint whatever we could reach from the ground. After a couple of hours of painting, David and I got bored, so we started goofing around."

"Just like the last time, huh, Grandpa?" I said.

"Yeah, I guess you could say David and I never learned. Anyway, all the paint back in those days was pretty nasty stuff. It was really hard to get off your hands, so we were supposed to be real careful not to get any on us or our clothes. Otherwise, our dad would have to use gasoline to clean it off. That's how bad the paint was.

"So on that day, I dipped my brush into the can of

paint, and before I went back to painting, I took the wet paintbrush and got it real close to David's hand. Then I lightly touched it so he got a little tiny drip of paint on his hand. We both thought that was funny and quietly laughed. We didn't want our dad to hear us goofing around.

"Next, David dipped his brush in the paint and held it real close to my chin. Then he lightly touched me with the wet paintbrush, leaving a little tiny streak of paint on my chin. Once again, we laughed and thought that was pretty funny. Of course, we were still being quiet, because our dad would have hollered at us if he'd known what we were doing."

I looked at my grandpa and shook my head. "I don't know, Grandpa. This is beginning to sound like you and David weren't very smart."

"Well, I guess we weren't. Now it was my turn to outdo David. I dipped my brush into the paint, and this time I thought I would show David up for sure. I stuck out my tongue and very gently touched it to the wet paint. I figured there was no way my brother was going to top that!

"After a couple of minutes though, David decided to do one better. He dipped his brush in the can of paint, and when he pulled it out, he opened his mouth real wide and pretended like he was going to put the whole brush in his mouth and eat it. And when he got the wet paintbrush almost inside his mouth, I did one of the meanest, rottenest things I've ever done to my little brother in my life. I hit David's hand, and the paint got all over the inside of his mouth."

"Eeeew!" I cried. "Are you serious, Grandpa?"

"I know! I know that was a rotten thing to do. But when you're ten years old, you don't always think before you act, do you? David screamed bloody murder, and when our dad heard him, he came down the ladder to see what happened. David stood there with the paintbrush in his hand and his mouth full of paint, trying to tell our dad what happened. But Dad couldn't understand what he was saying because David didn't want to close his mouth since it was full of paint. When he talked, his words sounded all garbled up.

"He tried to say, 'Jerry made me put paint in my mouth.' But it sounded like this: 'Erry ade ee oot aint n I outh.'

"My dad took David by the arm and dragged him into the garage, saying, 'I can't understand a word you're saying.' Then he poured a bunch of gasoline on a rag and told David to open his mouth. He took that stinky, gasoline-soaked rag and started cleaning the paint out of the inside of David's mouth. I wanted to laugh, but when I heard my brother crying and gagging from the taste of the paint and gasoline, I felt really bad for him. To this day, every time I open a new can of paint, I think about my brother, and I can't help but gag a little."

"So did you and your brother get in trouble *that* time?" I asked.

"Well, to be honest, I can't remember, but I'm sure you can understand why it was a long time after that before my brother would even speak to me again."

"That had to be the meanest trick you ever did, Grandpa."

"I have to admit it was a pretty mean trick, but I also did

one to your dad that I'm not very proud of. In some ways, that one ended up even worse."

"What could be worse than getting a mouthful of paint and then having it cleaned up with gasoline?" I really couldn't imagine what it might be.

"When your dad was eleven or twelve, he used to take really long showers, so I decided to teach him a lesson. So one time when your dad was taking a shower, I went down in the basement to turn off the hot water so your dad's shower would turn freezing cold. But I turned off the cold water by mistake, so instead of a cold shower, your dad got a burning hot shower. I didn't realize the water was hot until I heard him screaming at the top of his lungs.

"At first, I thought he was screaming because it was cold, so I started to laugh. Then I went upstairs and saw your grandma trying to get him to stop crying. When I saw how red his back was, I knew the joke wasn't very funny. Your grandma knew what I had done and chewed me out big time. It turned out that your dad was okay, but it was a long time before we did a trick on one another."

I thought about what my grandpa had just told me and felt bad for my dad. I spilled a cup of hot chocolate in my lap once and that really hurt. Of course, it spilled on my privates, which probably made it worse, but the hot water from the shower still must have hurt my dad a lot.

"So you see," Grandpa went on, "playing tricks on people can be funny, but you need to be careful about what you actually do or you might end up hurting someone like I did."

Embarrassing Things

My grandpa told me that, cuz he and his brother David were only a year apart when they were growing up, they did everything together.

"Everything?" I said.

"Well, we always sat next to each other at the dinner table. We sat next to each other when we watched TV and when we went to church. We slept in the same bed. We even got to take baths together. I guess you could say everything."

"You took baths together? I think I only took a bath with my brother when I was a baby. Did your other brothers and sisters take baths together?"

"With nine kids in the family, everybody had to take a bath with somebody else. That's just the way it was. I'm just glad I got to take a bath with David and not one of my sisters. And besides, with two of us, the bath wasn't so boring, and you could always blame the other person when Mom came in and saw water all over the floor.

"We used to have contests when we were taking a bath. One contest was to see who could stay under water the longest. I always won that. The other contest was a little more challenging. We used to see who could blow the most bubbles under water by farting. David had more gas than anyone in the world, so he always won that contest, especially when we had beans for supper."

"Okay, Grandpa, I know you have a lot of stories, but my next chapter is going to be about embarrassing things, so think about those kinds of stories, will ya?"

"Sure," he said, "have you got anything so far?"

"Well, the other day I had to go have a physical in order to go out for cross country. It was definitely embarrassing, so I thought I'd start with that. Did you ever have a physical, Grandpa?"

"Sure, everybody has to have a physical at one time or another." Then he asked, "Why was your physical so embarrassing?"

"Cuz, first of all, my mom was in the room with me the whole time, and second, cuz I had to take off all my clothes in front of the nurse . . . except for my boxers. Then the worst part was right at the end, after the doctor got done listening to my heart and my breathing and looking in my ears and down my throat and all that stuff. I thought he was going to say, 'Okay, go ahead and put your clothes back on,' but he didn't. Instead he had me lower my boxer shorts so he could check out the rest of me. If I had known that was going to be part of the physical, I never would have signed up for cross country in the first place."

Grandpa just laughed. "You got off pretty easy compared to my first physical. Mine turned out to be a real nightmare. And what made it more embarrassing was I was in ninth grade."

"Why did that make it worse?" I asked.

"Because when I was in ninth grade I *looked* like a sixth grader."

"What difference would that make?"

"Wait until you hear what happened then you'll understand. Believe me, it was definitely more embarrassing.

"I had to get my first physical because I went out for wrestling. I had to go there all by myself, and I'm still not sure if that was good or bad. The doctor's office was quite a long ways from our house, so I had to take the bus to get there. That was the easy part. When I got there, I climbed the three flights of steps to the third floor and was just about to go into the office when I decided I'd better check my armpits because it was a lot of work climbing up those steps, and I hoped I didn't have stinky, sweaty armpits for my first physical.

"I opened the door and walked into the reception area where there were three women who were probably waiting to see the doctor. All three of them looked up at me when I walked in. They kept looking at me as I walked over to the nurse, sitting at her desk in the corner of the room. I wondered if maybe I was in the wrong place. The nurse didn't look very friendly either. 'And what are you here for, young man?' the nurse said. I told her I had an appointment with Dr. Brown. After I said it, I realized how dumb it must have sounded since it was Dr. Brown's office. She looked frustrated and said, 'I realize you must have an appointment with Dr. Brown, but what is the appointment for?'

"I was a little embarrassed because it was a physical, so I whispered, 'A physical.'

"The nurse repeated, 'A physical!' in a rather loud voice, 'You must be Mr. Hinz.' All the ladies looked up from their magazines, and I felt my face flushing. This was not starting out very well.

"I waited for almost twenty minutes while the ladies kept looking over at me, until finally the mean looking nurse called out my name. We went down a short hallway, turned and went down another hallway, then turned again, and I thought we were going to end up right back where we started, but we went into a different room. The room was small and had another door on the opposite wall. I sat down in the chair next to the desk while the nurse wrote things down on some papers.

"Finally, she said, 'Jerry, I'm going to have you take off your . . . ' In that half-second before she finished her sentence, I turned all red and flushed. My heart started to pound. I thought for sure she was going to say, 'clothes.' She was going to tell me to take off my clothes right there in front of her. Then I heard the rest of her sentence: '. . . shoes so I can get your weight.' I was so relieved I only had to take off my shoes. After she took my weight, she wrote some more stuff down on the papers then went to the door to leave. Just before she stepped out, she turned around and said, 'The doctor will be in to see you in just a few moments. You'll need to take off all your clothes except your underwear.' "

"Sounds to me like your physical was pretty much the same as mine," I said. "So why do . . . "

My grandpa interrupted me, "Just wait, this is where it gets worse, much worse. I waited until she closed the door and left before I got undressed. I hoped she wouldn't be in the room when the doctor gave me my physical. I sat in the chair in just my underwear, facing the door on the other side of the room, waiting for the doctor. Finally, the door on the other side of the room opened, and I thought it was the doctor but it wasn't. It was the same nurse, and the door opened right into the waiting room where all the women were sitting. When she opened the door, all the women looked up and saw me sitting in just my underwear.

"When the nurse realized I was in that room, she said, 'Oh, Mr. Hinz, I'm sorry. I forgot you were in here.' Then she closed the door and left, but not before everyone in the waiting room got a good look at me in my underwear. This made me really nervous. I checked my armpits again, and this time they were pretty sweaty, so I picked up one of my dirty socks and wiped them off."

"Okay, Grandpa, I have to admit that would have been pretty embarrassing, but did the doctor . . . "

"Just wait! I'm not finished. A couple minutes later, the doctor finally came in. He asked me some questions about why I needed the physical and what grade I was in and then proceeded with the actual physical. After he looked in my ears and nose and listened to my heart and chest and all that other stuff, just like your physical, the doctor finally said he was going to have to check my . . . you know . . . down there. I didn't think it could be any worse than having all those women seeing me sitting there in my underwear, but it was. It turned out to be the worst part of all.

"When the doctor checked out my . . . you know . . . privates, he looked up at me and said, 'Did you say you were in *ninth* grade?' I turned all red in the face because I knew why the doctor asked me that. I may have been old enough for ninth grade but I definitely didn't look like a ninth grader."

I wasn't sure what my grandpa meant at first, but then it hit me. I started laughing and said, "Oh my gosh, Grandpa, I can't believe the doctor said that. You must have been soooo embarrassed."

"I told you my physical was more embarrassing."

After we stopped laughing, my grandpa said he remembered another incident that was pretty embarrassing—not as embarrassing as the physical, but still pretty embarrassing.

"When I was in seventh grade, I had to stay after school

and work on a project with a girl named Anna. I kind of liked her, but I never told her that."

"Was she your girlfriend, Grandpa?" I asked.

"No, but I wished she was. Anyway, I must have eaten something at lunch that gave me a lot of gas. I was trying to keep from passing the gas, but I knew that pretty soon I wouldn't be able to hold it back any longer. Then I remembered a trick that my dad showed me once. He showed me how to put my hands together and squeeze them just right so it would sound like a fart. Like this."

My grandpa put his hands together and squeezed them a few times and pretty soon they made a farting sound.

"That's cool," I said. "Will you show me how to do that?"

"Sure, maybe later. Anyway, Anna heard the noise and looked up from her drawing in disbelief, but before she could say anything I put my hands on the table and showed her my trick. When she heard my hands make the farting noise, she just said, 'That's gross,' and went on drawing.

"A couple of minutes later, I really had to pass some gas, so I put my hands under the table and pretended to make the farting noise with my hands again—only this time I really let one go. It was pretty loud. Anna didn't even look up from her work. She just said, 'You're not funny, I know you did that with your hands.' I smiled to myself, thinking I had gotten away with something. But after a few seconds went by, the smell came up from under the table. My face started to turn red, and pretty soon I knew that Anna smelled it, too, because she said, 'That wasn't your hands that made that noise, was it?' I was busted."

"That was a pretty good story, Grandpa. Now will you show me how to make the farting noise with my hands?"

"Let me tell you these other two stories first, before I forget them," he said. "This story is about your dad when he was just a little tyke, about two years old."

"Oh, good, I like to hear stories about my dad when he was little."

"This is when I took him up to the lake to visit *his* grandpa. Your dad was always a pretty active little kid, and we had to keep an eye on him all the time; otherwise, he would get in some kind of trouble. When we were up at the lake, he always wanted to go swimming every chance he could. But I wasn't crazy about taking him because our cabin was at the top of a big hill, and I would have to carry him down this long stairway just to get to the beach and then carry him back up when we were done."

"Didn't he know how to walk?" I asked.

"He knew how to walk all right, but the stairs were old and rickety, and I was afraid to let him walk on them by himself. Sometimes I would take him all the way down the steps to the beach, and after about five minutes in the water, your dad would say, 'I'm cold, Daddy, can we go back?' Then a little while later, he'd say, 'Can we go swimming, Daddy?' Of course, when we did go swimming since he was so little, I would have to stand there in the cold water with him. It was never any fun for me.

"Well, one nice, warm day, the two of us went down to

the beach for a swim, and as soon as your dad sat down in the water to play, he said, 'Daddy, I have to go potty.' There was no way I wanted to carry him all the way back up those steps just so he could go potty so I told him, 'When people go swimming in the lake and have to go pee, sometimes they just pee in the lake. After all, that's what the fish do.' Your dad said, 'Okay,' and went about playing with his bucket and shovel, and I thought he would just pee while he was sitting there in the water.

"I took my eyes off of him for barely a minute, and when I turned back to see what he was doing, he was standing in the water with his swimsuit down around his ankles, peeing in the lake. The people on the beach were all watching him, and I could tell they didn't think it was very funny. So I hollered, 'Brian, what do you think you're doing?' Of course, your dad just hollered back, 'You said, if I had to go potty, I should just go potty in the lake like the fish do.' "

"Are you serious, Grandpa? My dad just stood there and peed in the lake while everybody watched?"

"Well, he was only two years old, so I guess it wasn't that big of a deal for him. But *I* sure was embarrassed."

I wrote down the words "peed in the lake" so I wouldn't forget the story.

Then my grandpa said, "I have one more embarrassing story that happened to me, but it's so embarrassing that I'm not sure I should tell you. At least, I don't think it should end up in your book."

"Oh, come on, Grandpa, it can't be worse than when you had your first physical."

"Believe me, it was worse."

"Okay, Grandpa, if it's that bad I'll keep it out of the book, but you've gotta tell me what happened."

"This happened when I was about nine years old. Some of my friends and I didn't have anything to do one day, so I made up this stupid game for us to play on our front porch. When I was a kid, I used to always come up with some kind of stupid game to play because I didn't like to just sit around doing nothing. Usually the game would end with someone getting hurt. This time it was me."

"Was your brother playing, too?"

"He was playing, but he never got hurt—just me. Anyway, this stupid game was about trying different ways to jump off the porch without getting hurt. Each one of us had to make up a different way to jump. The first time we jumped, the first person made the rule that we had to stand on the rail and do a 360 degree twist in the air before we landed. So we all did. Then the next person said everyone had to touch their toes in the air. Everyone did that one, too. When it came to my turn, I said you had to sit on the rail with your feet out in front of you, then push off and do a full twist before you landed. Of course, since I made it up, I had to do it first."

"That sounds pretty easy, Grandpa," I said. "You couldn't have gotten hurt doing that."

"Just wait. Our porch was pretty old, just like the rest of

the house, and it needed to be painted. That meant some of the wood on the railing was bare and you could easily get slivers. I must have been sitting on a spot that was bare wood, because when I pushed off, I felt chunks of wood go right through my pants and into my rear end. I screamed bloody murder! Man, that really hurt. And when I hit the ground, I landed on my butt and drove the slivers even deeper. I reached back into my pants and pulled out a piece of the porch railing that was the size of a broken pencil, and I knew that there was more in there."

"That's sounds pretty painful, Grandpa, but it doesn't seem all that embarrassing."

"I know, but this is the embarrassing part. My mom was sitting on the porch at the time, and when she heard me scream all she said was, 'I'm glad it was you that got hurt and not one of your friends. Now get over here so I can have a look at you.'

"I stood in front of her for a couple of minutes, waiting for her to do something, but nothing happened. Finally, she said, 'I can't see through your pants, you know.' So I had to lower my pants right there on the front porch in front of God and everybody, and it wasn't *God* I was concerned about. It was the everybody else who was watching. All my friends stood there with big grins on their faces, waiting for me to drop my pants."

I started laughing, "Oh, my gosh, Grandpa, are you serious?"

"Yes, I'm serious, but that *still* wasn't the worst of it.

I had to lie down on her lap so she could get the rest of the slivers out. When everyone saw me with my rear end sticking up in the air, waiting for my mom to start digging the slivers out, they all started to giggle. Then my mom told my brother to go get a needle from her sewing basket. 'Make it a big one,' she said, and that made everyone laugh even louder. I was so embarrassed I wanted to cry, but I knew that would just make everyone laugh all the louder. I wished my mom would have taken me into the living room, and that way only my brothers and sisters would have been able to watch, not all of my friends, too.

"Finally, after about ten minutes of digging with a needle and pinching and pulling out the slivers, she said she was done. My brother was standing right next to me and said 'I think you missed one right there,' and poked me in the butt. Then he said, 'Oh, I guess it's only a freckle.'

"I tried to get up so I could pull up my pants but she put her hand on my back and said, 'Hold on there. We don't want you to get an infection. David, go upstairs and get some rubbing alcohol and a cotton ball.' This, of course, made everyone laugh one more time . . . everyone except me."

I couldn't stop laughing. That had to be the funniest story my grandpa ever told and, I had to agree, the most embarrassing.

Really Stupid Things

My grandpa gave me a ride home from a hockey game today, and we started talking about stupid things we had done. I told my grandpa about the stupid thing my brother, Cole, did in school yesterday.

"Cole said that everyone in his class needed a permission slip signed by their parents in order to go on a ski trip. His teacher had passed out the permission slips the day before, but Cole had lost his, so he asked the teacher for another one. Cole brought it back to his desk and signed our dad's name to it right there. Then the teacher began to collect the signed permission slips from the rest of the class. When he went by Cole, Cole handed him his slip, too. The teacher looked at Cole and rolled his eyes and said, 'How dumb do you think I am? I just gave you this to take home a minute ago.' Cole just said, 'Oh, yeah,' and took it back."

"Did Cole get in trouble?" Grandpa asked.

"No, he just brought it back today and put it on the teacher's desk. But you have to admit, that was pretty darn stupid. Did you ever do anything that stupid when you were in school?"

"I don't know if the things I did were *that stupid*, but I did do a couple of dumb things when I was in school. One time, when I was in first grade, I had to bring home my science project, and it was so big I had to use two hands to carry it. It was in the middle of the winter, and it was about ten degrees below zero outside. I only had a couple of blocks to go, but when I got home, I was cold and wanted to get in the house. I couldn't open the door because my hands were full, and I didn't want to set my science project down in the snow, so I tried to open the door with my mouth. The knob on the screen door was steel, so when I put my tongue on the door knob, it stuck to the knob like glue. I tried to holler for help but I couldn't because my tongue was in the way.

"After a couple of minutes of standing there and nobody coming to help me, I figured I better do something because I had to go to the bathroom and I didn't want to wet my pants and have that freeze up, too. So I did one of the dumbest things ever . . . I ripped my tongue off the steel doorknob. My tongue started bleeding and it hurt like heck. I ran up the stairs crying with my tongue hanging out because it hurt too much to pull it back in my mouth. When I got to the top of the steps, my mom saw me bleeding all over the floor so she hollered at me and told me to stick my tongue back in my mouth."

"Boy, Grandpa, trying to open up that door with your mouth was definitely a stupid thing to do. I think even I would have known better than to do that. Do you have any more?"

"Let's see . . . when I was bigger, my brother and I were getting ready for bed and we were both brushing our teeth. David finished first, and right before he left the bathroom, he splashed a little water in my face then ran upstairs to our bedroom in the attic. I heard him go upstairs so I filled my mouth up with water and went after him.

"I snuck up the stairs, knowing my brother would be hiding somewhere in the attic or in our bedroom. I went in the bedroom and looked behind the bed and in the closet. All of a sudden, the bedroom door slammed and David started running back down the steps. I ran out of the bedroom to catch him, and when he was half way down the steps, I spit the water at him, hoping to hit him in the back. But he turned the corner just in time, and the mouthful of water went all over the wall. The wall had real old wallpaper on it, and the wallpaper sucked up the water like a sponge and, of course, it made a great big mark on it.

"David ran the rest of the way down the stairs and, when he opened the door, he almost ran into our mom. She wanted to know why he was running, so she looked up into the attic stairway and saw me coming down after him.

Then she saw the big water mark on the wall, and I knew I was doomed.

"After a few minutes of interrogating David and me, she found out who spit the water on the wall and told me to go get my toothbrush and the bar of soap out of the bathtub. My punishment for spitting water on the wall was getting my mouth washed out with soap, but the worst part was all of my brothers and sisters got to watch. Sometimes having your brothers and sisters watch you getting punished is worse than the punishment itself."

"I don't know, Grandpa. I think getting my mouth washed out with a bar of soap that all my brothers and sisters used while they were taking a bath is worse. I mean just think about *that* for a minute."

Grandpa said, "Okay, okay! I get your point. Maybe you're right."

"Did you ever do anything stupid when you were in high school or when you were in the Navy?"

Grandpa said he remembered two pretty stupid things that happened to him in high school.

"The first one was my own fault. My high school was a pretty old building, and in the spring, a lot of the teachers would open up their classroom windows to let in some fresh air. Well, one day in March, it was pretty nice outside, but it had snowed pretty hard earlier and left about three inches of snow on the window ledges. My English teacher had opened the windows for the fresh air.

"My friend Denny and I were the first two kids in the

classroom, and when we noticed that the teacher hadn't come in yet, we reached out the window and made snow balls and threw them at some kids outside. When the bell rang, Denny threw some snow in my face and then ran to his seat. I quickly made a snowball then turned around and tossed it at Denny just as he got to his seat. I didn't notice that the teacher had already come into the room, and when Denny ducked, the snowball missed him but landed right on the teacher's desk and splattered snow all over him. Needless to say, I had to stay after school that day for hitting my teacher with a snowball."

"Well, that was pretty stupid, Grandpa. I hit one of my teachers with a snowball once, but we were outside and our class was having a snowball fight. That's a little different."

Grandpa continued, "The other thing that happened to me in school wasn't really my fault but, I still felt pretty darn stupid. I had to go to the bathroom really bad, and the worst part was I had to go number two. Nobody ever wanted to go number two at school because the bathroom stalls didn't have any doors on them; so when you were sitting there, everybody in the bathroom could see you."

"I know just what you mean, Grandpa. It's still the same in school today. Nobody ever wants to go number two at school. One day I pretended I had a bad headache so I could go to the nurse just to use her bathroom cuz I had to go number two. Her bathroom has a door that you can lock."

My grandpa went on, "Well, this one day just before lunch, I had to go really bad, so I waited around in the bathroom until everybody had left then quickly sat down to go.

"All of a sudden the bathroom door opened and someone hollered, 'Is anyone in here?' I didn't say anything because I didn't want anyone to know I was going number two. Next thing, the door closed and then I heard something that sounded like the lock turning. All of a sudden, I realized that whoever hollered must have been a teacher and he just locked the door. Back in those days, they used to have to lock the bathrooms during the lunch periods because, if they didn't, kids would go in and smoke. I finished my business and rushed over to the door. Sure enough, it was locked."

I laughed and asked, "Were you scared? Did you wonder if you'd ever get out?"

Grandpa answered, "No, I don't remember being scared. But I do remember standing next to the door, wondering what to do. I didn't want to pound on the door, because if a student heard me and found out I was locked in the bathroom during lunch, the word would be all over the school and everyone would think I was the stupidest freshman there. So I decided to just wait until a teacher opened the door for the next lunch. When it was time for someone to finally open the door, I went back to the furthest stall and stayed in there until a bunch of kids came in then I just walked out like nothing happened. The only problem was I was hungry for the rest of the day because I missed my lunch."

"Unbelievable! Grandpa, how stupid was that?"

My grandpa told me he did a number of stupid things when he was in the Navy but he said he could only tell me one. He said he couldn't tell me the others until I got older.

"One time when I was in Hawaii, I and a few of my buddies went to a beach to go swimming. The beach was on the other side of the island, so there weren't very many people there. We didn't have any swimsuits, so we decided to swim in our boxer shorts. It really wasn't a big deal because the other people weren't very close to us, so there was no way they would be able to tell we were swimming in our underwear."

I told my grandpa, "I've gone swimming in my boxer shorts plenty of times. There's nothing stupid about that."

"That wasn't the stupid part," he said. "Let me finish. The beach that we were at had some pretty big waves, so we all decided to go body-surfing. We had to go out kind of far in order to catch some good waves, and that meant we had to swim through the waves to get out there.

"Well, when I was in the Navy, I wasn't very big. In fact, I was actually kind of small, like you. So my boxer shorts didn't fit very well. They were at least two sizes too big for me. And every time I dove into a wave, I could feel my boxer shorts go down to my knees.

"We were out there pretty far, waiting for a big wave to ride back to shore. Sure enough, when I dove through one of the waves, it took my boxers completely off. I looked and looked everywhere, but we were in water over our heads, and I couldn't find them anywhere. When I told my buddies what had happened, all they did was laugh and ask me how I was going to get back to my clothes. I didn't know what I was going to do because our clothes were about fifty yards from the edge of the water, and now there were more people on the beach, and some were sitting right in front of our clothes. To get to my clothes, I'd have to run right past them . . . naked."

"Oh man, Grandpa, I can't wait to hear how you got out of this one."

"When we all got back in the shallow water, my buddies got out of the water and kept coaxing me to come on out! They thought the whole thing was pretty funny, but I just stayed in the shallow water. I didn't want to run across the beach without anything on. Since we didn't have any towels with us, there really wasn't anything they could bring me to cover up with. Finally, one of my buddies brought me my undershirt and told me that was the best he could do. I knew that the undershirt was too small to wrap around me like a towel, so I turned it upside down and put one of my legs into each one of the arms and pulled it up just like a pair of shorts. It worked well enough to get me over to my clothes where I could put on my shirt and pants."

"You probably better stick to using a swimsuit, Grandpa," I said.

Church Days

I was working on my book today and didn't know how to spell one of my grandpa's words, so I asked my mom how to spell it.

"Mom," I hollered, "How do you spell *bejeebers*?"

"Spell what?" she asked.

"You know, *bejeebers*. Grandpa said this guy scared the bejeebers out of him, and I've been going over my notes for my book, and I need to know how to spell it."

"Bejeebers!" she said, "I've never heard of it. I don't even think that's a word."

"Oh, it's a word all right. Grandpa said it when he was telling me one of his stories, so I'm sure it's a word."

"Well, if you're so sure it's a word, then maybe you'd better call your grandpa and he can tell you how to spell it. And I told you before, Luke, you can't believe everything your grandpa tells you."

That's the one part of this writing that I'm not too crazy about: the spelling and the punctuation. My grandpa said, if I was the only one who was ever going to read my book, then I wouldn't have to worry about the spelling. But if I'm going to let anyone else read it, then I'd better work on the grammar a little. He said, "You don't want everyone thinking you're a dummy, do you?" or something like that. Then we started to talk about when my grandpa went to church.

Grandpa said he went to a Catholic church when he was growing up, but when he was growing up, church was lot different.

"Back when I was a kid, they were stricter than they are today," he said.

"What do you mean, 'they were stricter'?" I asked.

"Well, we could never miss going to church on Sunday, no matter what. Even if you threw up the night before and still felt sick in the morning, my mom would make you go to church. The only one in our family who ever got to stay home from Sunday mass was my brother Jim because he had asthma."

"Asthma! That's when you have a hard time breathing, right?"

"That's right."

"I had a kid with asthma in my gym class this year. One time when we had to run a mile, the kid forgot his puffer thing . . . "

Grandpa interrupted, "You mean his inhaler."

"Oh yeah, inhaler, that's what it was called. Anyway, when he finished the mile, he sat down on the grass and leaned forward and started wheezing and trying to catch his breath, but he couldn't. He sounded really bad . . . kinda like an old person snoring with a whistle stuck in his throat, only scarier and louder."

"That's the way it was with my brother. Sometimes when he had a really bad attack, he would have to go to the hospital. I guess asthma was bad enough to miss church once in a while.

"This one time my brother was sick all night on a Saturday, and I knew there was no way he was going to have to go to church, so I told my mom that I would stay home with him so she could go to church. My mom said that was very nice of me, and she and my dad and the rest of the family went off to church. I thought I had pulled a fast one; but when my mom got home, she told me there was just enough time for me to get ready and go to the ten o'clock mass. I was really ticked off, because not only would I still have to go to church, but I would have to walk to church instead of getting a ride in the car like everyone else did.

"When I was upstairs getting ready for church, I was so mad that I decided I would just pretend to go to church and go to the playground instead but that idea got shot down. When I was walking out the door, my mother said, 'Don't forget to bring home the Sunday bulletin.' I couldn't get the bulletin without going to church. I never stayed home to watch my stupid brother again."

Then Grandpa told me what it was like when his whole family went to church. He said it was a real circus.

"We always went to the early mass because not very many people were there, and that way if we did something dumb or embarrassing, not too many people knew about it.

"It was pretty funny when we first got there and started to file into the pews because my mom wanted us to sit in a certain order. She didn't want David and me to sit together because we screwed around too much, and she didn't want David and Mary to sit next to each other because they fought all the time, and someone had to sit between Jim and Dad to keep the two of them awake, and nobody wanted to sit next to my sister, Donna, because she was a brat. So every time one of us would try and get into the pew and sit where we wanted to, my mom would grab that person by the neck and pull him or her out and put someone else in. Anyway, it all looked pretty funny."

"How many of you were there?" I asked.

"There were nine kids plus my mom and dad so you can see why it looked pretty funny.

"Another funny part of church was when my dad fell asleep. When he dozed off, he snored; and when he snored, it was loud—*really loud*. He usually fell asleep during the sermon."

"You mean the part where the priest does all the talking and it's always really boring. At least our priest is anyway. If your priest was anything like ours, I can see why your dad fell asleep."

"Well, he sure wasn't interesting! Anyway, one time my dad was snoring so loud that I thought even the priest could even hear him all the way up in the front of the church. My mom was getting mad because she wasn't sitting close enough to my dad to wake him up so he just kept snoring away. I was sitting behind my dad and Mom looked over at me and motioned for me to hit my dad on the back of the head to wake him up. I wasn't too crazy about whacking my dad on the back of the head, but my mom kept waving at me to do it, so I finally did."

"You smacked your dad on the head right there in church?" I asked.

"Yup, and I must have hit my dad pretty hard because he turned around and looked at me like he was going to give me a beating right there in church. I never did get a beating, but my dad was pretty mad at me for awhile. After it was all over, I used to brag to my brothers and sisters that I was the only one who ever got to hit our dad and get away with it."

I laughed and said, "If my dad ever fell asleep in church, it would be really funny. You wanna know why?" Before Grandpa could ask why, I said, "Cuz he drools when he sleeps. I can just see him sitting there with a big old wet spot in the middle of his shirt."

We both laughed. Then my grandpa told me some other things about being a Catholic when he was a kid.

"Back in those days," he said, "Catholics couldn't eat meat on Fridays, so my mom always had to try and make some kind of supper that would fill us up but without meat. My dad went fishing a lot, so sometimes we had fish—fish didn't count as meat—but he didn't catch enough fish to have it every Friday. So my mom had to think of other things that didn't have meat in it. Some of them were pretty strange."

"Like what?" I asked.

"One of the things we had pretty often was Egg Spaghetti," he said.

"Egg Spaghetti! What the heck is Egg Spaghetti?"

"Well, the way my mom made it was like this: She would boil up a big pot of spaghetti noodles and then put the pasta in a huge frying pan and crack a couple of eggs into it. She would fry it for a while until the eggs were cooked right into the spaghetti, and just like that, you had Egg Spaghetti. I know it sounds really dumb, but it was actually pretty good."

"I'm sure glad I didn't live back then cuz I am pretty sure I wouldn't have liked it."

Then Grandpa said, "Another thing the Catholics had to do every now and then was go to church on Holy Days. Most of the time, the Holy Days were during the week which meant I would have to go to church before school. I actually thought that was pretty cool because it meant I would get to bring my breakfast to school and eat it in the classroom before school started."

"So why didn't you just eat your breakfast before you went to church?"

"Back then the church had a rule that said you couldn't eat anything before going to church."

"Sounds like a pretty dumb rule to me. What was so cool about eating breakfast in your classroom?"

"I always got to bring a hard-boiled egg and toast for breakfast. When I peeled the egg, all the girls said it stunk and made them sick, so I would eat the egg real slow just to make them mad. One time the egg smelled so bad my teacher made me go in the hall and eat it. There was one problem though, the egg always gave me stinky gas; so in the afternoon, I would have to hold back a bunch of gas because I didn't want to just let one go right there in the classroom."

Then Grandpa told me that the worst part about being a Catholic and going to Catholic school was going to confession.

He explained, "Confession is a little like getting caught doing something bad at home and having to say you're sorry; and then getting punished for doing it, even if you got away with it in the first place. You had to go in this little room and tell the priest what you did wrong, and then he would tell you to say a bunch of prayers for your punishment."

"How many prayers would he make you say?"

"That depended on how bad you were. If you just called your sister a butthead or something like that, you only got a small punishment. But my brother used to steal money from my dad; so when he went to confession, it took him a half an hour to say all his prayers.

"Once in a while, the priest would give me a different kind of punishment. It wasn't like the priest could ground you or take away your TV time or anything like that; but one time the priest told me I had to do five nice things to my sister for my punishment because I called her a *stinky* butthead. I didn't think that was fair at all. I would rather have been grounded than be nice to my sister.

"The other bad part about confession was that all the kids in my class would stand in line right next to the confessional, which was this little, tiny room you had to go in to tell your sins to the priest. One of the priests was real old and couldn't hear very well, so you had to speak real loud when you told him your sins. All the kids that were waiting in line could hear you, so they knew what your sins were. And sometimes the priest would holler at you, and then all the kids in line would be giggling when you came out. I definitely didn't like confession."

Grandpa's School Days

My grandpa said he not only went to a Catholic church but also a Catholic grade school when he was my age. I asked him what the heck a grade school was. He said it was the same as a elementary school, only it went from kindergarten through eighth grade instead of kindergarten through fifth grade. I wanted to ask him if that meant the kids back then were dumber cuz they had to go through eight grades of elementary school instead of just five grades, like at my elementary school . . . but I didn't. I don't think my grandpa would have thought that was very funny. My grandpa said that his Catholic grade school was a whole lot different than my elementary school.

He said, "One of the biggest differences was that we had nuns for teachers instead of just regular old teachers."

"What's a nun?" I asked.

"A nun is like a regular teacher, only meaner. They were all women and wore black and white uniforms that smelled kind of like mothballs. In fact, their clothes sort of made them look like penguins. The black part was a dress that had long sleeves with big openings at the end, so when they folded their arms, they would tuck their hands in the sleeves. That way it looked like they didn't have any hands. They wore a belt that was made out of beads as big as marbles with a cross on the end of it. The dress went all the way to the floor so you couldn't see their shoes. The white part was a funny looking bib that went around their necks—that was the part that made them look like penguins. And they wore this black veil with a white crown on their heads. That made them look like a cross between a penguin and a scary nurse. Oh yeah, and they all had funny names."

"You're right, Grandpa, they sure don't sound like regular old teachers. What was funny about their names?"

"They all had two first names, and some of them were boy names. There was Sister Patrick Mary and Sister Katherine Cecelia and Sister John Joseph. This one year, I had Sister Mary Ellen. Sister Mary Ellen was really, really big, so some of the sixth graders used to call her Sister Mary Elephant behind her back. I heard that this one kid got caught calling her that, and she flunked him back to the fourth grade."

"Are you serious, Grandpa? Was that really true?"

"I don't know for sure, but you can bet *I* never called her Sister Mary Elephant."

Then I asked, "Was there anything different about the nuns besides how goofy they looked and their names?"

He said, "Let me tell you a couple of stories about what the nuns were like back when I went to school, and you can decide."

Grandpa rubbed his chin and went on. "There was no such thing as privacy at my school, not even when you went to the bathroom. One day I had a lot of gas—it must have been one of the days I had a hard-boiled egg for breakfast. Anyway, I was trying all morning not to pass gas in the classroom because I knew, if I let one go in the classroom and Sister Mary Ellen heard it or smelled it, she would probably make me stay after school and write a hundred times on the board, *I will not pass gas in the classroom.*"

"Why would you have to write it on the board?" I asked.

"That's one of the things they did back then if you got in trouble . . . you had to write stuff over and over on the board. One time, my buddy Fredrick and I were talking in class, so Sister Mary Ellen made us stay after and write our first, middle and last names on the board a hundred times. I thought it was pretty funny because my name, Jerry Hinz, only has nine letters, and I don't have a middle name. My friend's name, which is Fredrick Wellington Romanowski III, has thirty-one letters. Just when I thought I got away with something, Sister Mary Ellen told me that, since I didn't have a middle name, I would have to write *Jerry I Don't Have A Middle Name Hinz.* I didn't think it was very funny after that.

"Anyway, what was I talking about?"

"You were just getting ready to far . . . I mean pass some gas in the classroom."

"Oh yeah, I had to pass some gas. Back then, the whole class always went to the bathroom together, so when it was finally time for my class to go to the bathroom, I figured I could finally get rid of the gas without worrying about Sister Mary Ellen. But wouldn't you know it, she walks right into the boys' bathroom with the class. I couldn't hold it back any longer, so I finally let it go right in front of her, and it made a big noise. When I turned around and looked at her, she just shook her head and said, 'Was that really necessary, Mr. Hinz?' I wanted to tell her, 'Heck yeah, it was necessary. I've been holding that in all morning,' but I knew better, so I just hung my head and said, 'Sorry.' "

"How come the nuns went in the boys' bathroom in the first place?" I asked.

"Because they wanted to make sure we didn't goof around. Some of the eighth graders got caught opening up the windows and throwing balled-up, wet, paper towels at the kids on the playground, and after that the nuns went into the bathrooms to make sure the boys just did their business and got out of there."

"Were all the nuns mean and crabby?" I asked.

"Most of them were, as far as I can remember. My sister said she had a nun who was really nice to her, but I think that was because she always sucked up by staying after school and washing the chalkboards or coming to school early and taking down all the chairs off the desks. I even heard a rumor that she polished that nun's shoes. I don't know if that's true, but I wouldn't have put it past my sister. And I do know all the nuns I had were mean."

"Which one was the meanest?" I asked.

"The meanest nun in the whole school was Sister Katherine Cecelia. She was my fourth-grade teacher. The reason I think she was the meanest is because she tried to flunk me."

"Really, are you serious, Grandpa? She actually tried to flunk you?"

"That's right," he said. "In fourth grade, they used to give you a reading test to see what grade level you could read at. When the test results came back, Sister Katherine Cecelia called me up to her desk and told me that I was only reading at a third-grade level, so I might not pass fourth grade.

"When I heard this, my heart skipped a beat, and my face turned ashen white. I was scared to death. I thought I was going to faint right on the spot. Sister Katherine Cecelia smiled at me and said, 'You'd better sit down. You don't look so good.' What would all my friends say if they knew I wasn't going to pass fourth grade? And what would my mom and dad do to me? I wondered if they might ground me for the whole summer."

"Oh man, Grandpa, if I got news like that, I don't know what I would have done. So did she flunk you?"

"Just wait a minute," he said. "I went home and told

my mom what my teacher told me, but Mom didn't seem very concerned. She said that my teacher was probably just trying to scare me so I would do better at reading. I felt a lot better because my mom was also a teacher, and if she wasn't concerned, why should I be?"

"So she didn't flunk you, right?"

"Hold on, I didn't say that. When I went back to school the next day, Sister Katherine Cecelia called me up to her desk and asked me if I talked to my mom about my reading. I told her yes and then told her what my mom said about just trying to scare me. I probably shouldn't have told her that, because when I got my report card on the last day of school, it said DID NOT PASS FOURTH GRADE right on the front."

"So you *did* flunk fourth grade! Oh, my gosh, my grandpa flunked fourth grade. I can't wait to tell Cole that our grandpa flunked fourth grade. That had to be like the end of the world for you!"

"Will you quit interrupting and let me finish?" I could tell my Grandpa was getting frustrated cuz he flares his nose when he's frustrated, and both nostrils were big enough for a tennis ball. My grandpa took a big breath and went on.

"Needless to say, I cried all the way home. All I could think about was being grounded for the summer and having to stay in my room and read all day and never getting to go outside and play. My brothers and sisters would be teasing me all the time, calling me 'dummy' or 'flunky' or something like that. And having to face my friends when they found out would be unbearable. Then I had the worst thought of all: 'what if I got Sister Katherine Cecelia for a teacher again the next year?' That made me cry even more.

"When I got home, my mom could tell I had been crying and asked me what was wrong. I couldn't say anything. I just pulled out my report card and handed it to her. She read it and got really angry. At first I thought she was mad at me, but after a couple of minutes, I realized she wasn't mad at me, she was mad at Sister Katherine Cecelia."

"Why would she be mad at her? She wasn't the one who was flunking, you were," I said.

"That's what I thought, but she kept saying, 'Did not pass fourth grade? Just who does she think she is?' Then she said we would go visit with Sister Katherine Cecelia and straighten this whole matter out.

"I was a little bit worried because I had never seen my mom this mad before. I'd hoped she wouldn't do anything that would get me in even more trouble. I even wondered if Sister Katherine Cecelia could flunk me two grades if my mom made her mad enough.

"The next day when we went to school, my mom didn't say anything to me the whole way there. I sat out in the hall while Mom talked to my teacher. Once in a while, a kid that I knew would go by and look at me and giggle because he knew I was in trouble. Back then, kids loved it when somebody else was in trouble, even if they were your friend."

"Yeah, I know what you mean," I said, "The other day

I was sitting in the office waiting for my mom to pick me up, and every kid who went by looked at me and laughed. The next day they all asked me what kind of trouble I was in just cuz I was sitting in the office."

Grandpa went on, "Well, finally, my mom opened the door and told me to come in so Sister Katherine Cecelia could tell me what they decided. The first thing I noticed was that Sister Katherine Cecelia had been crying. '*Oh wow!*' I thought. '*My mom made Sister Katherine Cecelia cry!*' I couldn't wait to get home and tell my brother that Mom made one of the nuns cry.

"Sister Katherine Cecelia sort of apologized for putting DID NOT PASS on my report card and said that she only wanted me to realize how important it was that I kept up on my reading. Then she told me to work on improving my reading over the summer and that I *would* be going into fifth grade next year like everybody else."

"So you didn't flunk fourth grade after all," I said.

"Nope. My mom told me I wasn't supposed to tell anyone about what happened. It was supposed to be our secret. I told her, 'Okay,' but as soon as I got home I told my brother, David, about how our mom made Sister Katherine Cecelia cry."

"Well, all I can say is you were pretty darn lucky, Grandpa."

Then my grandpa told me another school story. It was the most embarrassing story I've ever heard. It was even worse than my grandpa's physical or the time he got slivers in his butt. Fortunately, for my grandpa, it didn't happen to him. It happened to one of his classmates.

"This happened to a kid in my class named Terry. Our class was using the bathroom after gym class, and there weren't any nuns in there to watch us because the gym teacher, Mr. Wetsox, didn't really care if we goofed around in the bathroom.

"I had just finished going to the bathroom and went over to wash my hands when I thought I heard someone crying. Everyone had left except me and Terry. Terry didn't have a lot of friends, but I liked him for one main reason. He was the smallest kid in my class. If Terry wasn't in my class, then I would have been the smallest kid in class. I looked over at the urinals and saw that Terry was standing there with his head down.

"When I asked him what was wrong, Terry didn't say anything, but every now and then I thought I heard him sniffle. So I went over to him and asked him if he was okay.

"Finally, after a couple of minutes, Terry turned away from the urinal and faced me so I could see what was wrong. He had somehow zippered part of his you-know-what in his zipper. I told Terry to stay right there, and I would go get help. I knew there was no way I was going to try and fix that!"

I started to laugh, but my grandpa kept right on telling the story so I stopped. I didn't want to miss any of *this* story.

"I ran out of the bathroom and down the hall as fast as I could, hoping to find Mr. Wetsox. When I turned the corner, I ran into Sister Mary Ellen. Since she was a pretty big nun, it was like running into the wall. I started to fall, so I grabbed the beads around her waist and almost pulled her down on top of me. For a split second, I was lying on the floor, looking up at her trying to catch her balance, and I thought, '*If she falls, I'm going to get squished like a bug.*' Fortunately for me, she didn't. I must have also caught hold of part of her head veil, because when she stood back up, the thing on top of her head was tipped to the side, and she looked like a lopsided penguin—a really big, lopsided penguin. I wanted to laugh but I knew better.

"She grabbed me by the shirt collar and asked me what I was doing running in the hall. I told her about what happened to Terry in the bathroom, and that I was going to get Mr. Wetsox because he'd probably know what to do better than anybody."

"Was he the only man in the whole school?" I asked.

"That's right," Grandpa said, "There was no such thing as a man nun, and all we had were nuns in our school, except for Mr. Wetsox."

Grandpa scratched his head then continued, "She just shook me a couple of times and said, 'Show me what you're talking about.' I didn't want to because I knew how embarrassing it would be for Terry, but I knew I didn't have any choice either. So I took her into the boys' bathroom. Terry was standing right where I'd left him. When Sister Mary Ellen saw Terry and asked him what was wrong, Terry turned three different shades of red and turned away from her so she couldn't see. I tried to help him out and said, 'Maybe I better go get Mr. Wetsox,' and turned like I was going to leave but she just said, 'That won't be necessary.' Then she bent down and turned Terry around so she could see what was wrong. Terry went from having a bright red face to a chalk white one. Next she looked at Terry and said, 'Now, this is only going to hurt for a second.' It looked like she was smiling when she said it. Then she took the zipper in one hand and Terry's you-know-what in the other hand, and I thought poor old Terry was going to pass out. In one quick move, Terry was free. I thought Terry was going to scream, but he never made a sound. He must have been too scared or too embarrassed to do anything. All I could think of was how glad I was that didn't happen to me."

"Are you serious, Grandpa? Did that really happen?" I asked.

"It sure did, and to this very day, I still feel bad for Terry."

Then I asked, "If that had happened to you instead of Terry, would you have still told me the story?"

"No way!"

"I thought so," I said, and we both laughed.

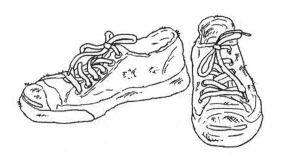

Stinky Stevens

I was riding my bike over to my friend Johnny's house today and decided to stop at my grandpa's house for a few minutes cuz Johnny only lives about a half a block away from there. Johnny likes my grandpa and pretends that my grandpa is one of his own grandpas. He told me he goes over to see my grandpa all the time. I think the real reason Johnny stops over at my grandpa's is cuz my grandma always gives him a can of pop and something to eat when he comes over. My grandma's real nice that way.

The reason I went over to see my grandpa was to tell him how I was coming along on my book and to tell him what happened at school today. Something pretty funny happened, and I was sure my grandpa would want to hear about it. I wanted to see if he thought it would be okay to put in my book.

When I got there, my grandpa was in the backyard, working in his garden. He was singing to his flowers, so I stood there for a minute and listened to him. I tried not to laugh, but it was hard cuz, when he sings to his flowers, he sings pretty loud. He told me once that singing to the flowers makes them grow more.

"Grandpa, do you want to take a break from all that singing? I got a story I want to tell you."

"Oh, you startled me! Hi, Luke. Sure, why don't you go downstairs and get us a can of pop first."

When I came back with the pop, Grandpa was sitting on the steps waiting for me.

"So how was school today?" he said.

"Boring, as usual, but something kind of funny happened, and I thought you might want to hear about it.

"There's this eighth grader named Vince—everyone calls him Vinnie—and he thinks he's really cool. He wears all kinds of chains and earrings and even has his hair spiked and painted green, and his pants are always sagging lower than anyone's in the whole school . . . "

Grandpa stopped me. "Wait a minute. What do you mean sagging? What was wrong with his pants?"

"You know—sagging," I said. "He wears them down real low so you can see his boxer shorts."

"Yeah, I guess I have seen that. I just thought they were that low because the kid didn't have a belt. Go on."

"Anyway, he's actually a pretty cool kid, but sometimes he just looks a little weird. Well, today he wore a pair of boxer shorts that had a hole in them; so when his pants were sagging real low, you could actually see his butt crack.

"After lunch a bunch of kids were hanging around in the hallway, waiting for the bell to ring, and Vinnie was with them. His pants were sagging really low and the kids were trying to see how much of his butt was showing. Then one of Vinnie's friends gave him a bottle of Mountain Dew and told him to put it in his pocket and bring it to his next class so they could share it. The bottle was pretty big and heavy; so when Vinnie put it in his pocket and started to walk down the hall, his pants fell all the way down to the floor. Vinnie was standing in the hall in just his boxer shorts with the big hole in them."

"That must have looked pretty funny. Were there any girls there?"

"Oh, yeah, there were girls, too. The really funny part came next. The cap on the Mountain Dew wasn't screwed on tight, so when Vinnie's pants hit the floor, the Mountain Dew got shook up and started squirting all over Vinnie's pants. Vinnie didn't want to pull up his pants cuz the Mountain Dew was still spraying all over. But he didn't want to stand there in just his underwear with everybody laughing either. Lucky for him, the boys' bathroom was across the hall. Vinnie went in there, and I don't know what happened to him after that."

Grandpa laughed and said, "Next time, maybe he'll think twice before he wears his pants so low."

Then I asked, "Did kids ever wear pants that sagged back when you went to school?"

Grandpa said, "If we would have worn our pants sagging when I went to school, we would have been sent home. In fact, if you didn't have a belt on, they sent you home; and if your pants had a tear in them, they sent you home; and if a girl wore a skirt that was above her knee, they would send her home."

I couldn't believe it and said, "So nobody ever sagged back when you went to school, Grandpa?"

"Nope, I'm afraid sagging is something your generation came up with."

Then Grandpa told me another story about a prank he did when he was in grade school. It had to do with a pair of stinky tennis shoes.

My grandpa said there was this kid named "Stinky" Stevens in his seventh-grade class. His real name was Donnie, but everybody called him Stinky Stevens because he had the smelliest feet in the whole world.

Right away I said, "They couldn't have been worse than Cole's feet after he gets done skating. Cole's feet would have been no contest for Stinky Stevens. The other day when Cole got back from rollerblading, he took off his skates and tried to get our dog Sassy to play with one of his socks. When Sassy smelled the socks, she ran outside."

Grandpa just laughed and said, "When a new kid came to school, we would take bets on how long the new kid could sit next to Stinky Stevens with his shoes off before the new kid started gagging. Nobody ever made it past three minutes."

"So what was this prank you did?"

"I'm getting to it, now just hang on. In seventh grade, we had gym every day of the week, so we always had to have a pair of tennis shoes at school. Most kids just kept their tennis shoes in the coat room in the back of the classroom. At first, Stinky Stevens kept his back there with everybody else, but it wasn't long before nobody would go in the coat room to change their shoes when he was there. In the afternoon, the smell from those tennis shoes would start to work its way into the classroom, and pretty soon some kid would tell the teacher he needed to go to the nurse because he had an upset stomach. Our teacher finally had to tell Stinky to change his shoes in the boys' locker room and leave his tennis shoes there. She didn't want them in the classroom anymore."

"Wow! Those really must have been bad," I said.

"They were so bad Stinky was supposed to bring them home every Friday and clean them so they wouldn't be so stinky on Monday, but he never did. He'd take them home, all right, but they would stink just as bad, if not worse, when he came back on Monday.

"One time we had a substitute teacher on a Monday, so we decided to play a trick on her."

"Is this the prank?"

"Yes, now just listen. When Stinky came in on Mondays, he was supposed to bring his shoes right to the locker room and leave them there. Since we had a substitute, I told Stinky he should leave his shoes in the coat room so we could play a trick on the substitute. When it was time for our class to go to the bathroom, I was the last one in line; and while everyone was gone, I went into the coat room and got Stinky's tennis shoes and put them in the teacher's desk.

"When we got back from the bathroom and the substitute sat down at her desk, she knew there was something wrong. She kept turning her head and wrinkling her nose, trying to figure out what the smell was and where it was coming from. She walked around her desk, sniffing. When she picked up the trash can and smelled the inside of that, I almost started laughing. She even put her head under the desk to see if the smell was coming from there. Since Stinky and I were the only ones to know about the tennis shoes, everyone else wondered what was wrong with the substitute.

"Finally, she sat back down at the desk and started opening the drawers, smelling inside each drawer as she opened them. When she got to the drawer that had the tennis shoes, she took a big whiff and almost fell out of her chair. I had to put my hand over my mouth to keep from laughing out loud. Then she pulled out the tennis shoes and held them at arm's length, pinching her nose with the other hand. 'Whose tennis shoes are these?' she said.

"Stinky was a pretty smart kid so he jumped out of his desk and said, 'Oh, you found my tennis shoes! I've been looking for them all morning. I must have forgotten to put them away last Friday, and our teacher put them in her desk so she would remember to give them to me today.' The look on the substitute's face made me think that she didn't believe a word Stinky was saying. I was sure we would get in trouble, but we didn't. The substitute never did mention it to our teacher."

"You and Stinky got pretty lucky that time, huh, Grandpa," I said.

The Biggest Dare

Grandpa told me that one of the things they used to do all the time when he was a kid was "dare" someone to do something.

He said, "Usually two kids would sit around and make dares for each other when they were bored and didn't have anything better to do. Those dares were never a very big deal."

"Like what?" I asked.

"Oh, I might dare one of my friends to ring Mrs. Goldberg's doorbell. She knew every kid in the neighborhood; and if she saw who did it, she'd tell your mom in a minute. Or they might dare me to steal an apple from Mr. Turdee's apple tree. You had to climb over his fence to get one; and if he saw you, he'd come out and chase you with a broom. One time I stayed over at a friend's house and we slept on the front porch. He dared me to run around the house in just my underwear. Then I dared him to do it naked. Before you knew it, we were both running through the neighborhood without any clothes on."

I laughed and said, "Don't tell my mom this, but I did that just last week on a bet. Only I had to ride my bike without anything on. It was at night so nobody saw me . . . I hope."

Grandpa continued, "If you ever did a dare in front of a bunch of kids, then everyone thought you were really cool. One year at camp, I gave this kid named Tim a dare and tricked him pretty good. We were all ten- and eleven-year-olds, so we were pretty immature and always playing tricks on each other.

"Tim was the biggest eleven-year-old in the world. He looked like he was sixteen. And he was the most daring kid in our cabin. Tim would do more dares than anyone. One day after we finished swimming and we were changing back into our clothes, I dared Tim to go outside without any clothes on—and without a towel—to hang up his swimsuit on the clothesline. The clothesline was about thirty feet from the back of the cabin. Now that doesn't seem like a very big dare, since there were only boys at the camp, but it was visiting day, and there were families walking around the camp that day. Tim must have forgotten about the families and said, 'Sure, I'll do it, that's no big deal.'

"Before I made the dare, I saw two girls standing by a cabin a short distance from ours. Tim obviously hadn't seen them. He went out the cabin door with nothing on and hurried to the clothes line. When he started to tie the suit on the line, I hollered, 'Hey Tim, you forgot your towel. Do you need it?' When the two girls heard me holler at Tim, they looked over and saw him standing there naked and screamed.

"When Tim saw the two girls, he ran back to the cabin yelling, 'Hinz, I'm going to kill you!' I, of course, took off running, knowing that Tim wouldn't chase me without any clothes on. The girls must not have told anybody, because Tim never got in trouble; and since Tim didn't get in trouble, he never did beat up on me. As far as I was concerned, that was the real dare."

I asked my grandpa, "Was that the best dare you ever saw or did?"

"No, that one was pretty good but the best one ever was with Stinky Stevens."

"It must have something to do with his shoes," I said.

"Actually it had to do with his socks. One time Stinky Stevens dared anyone to put one of his socks in their mouth and keep it there for a minute . . . and, Stinky said, 'If you do it right after I get done running around in gym class when my feet are all sweaty, I'll give you fifty cents.' I thought pretty seriously about doing it, myself, since there was money involved."

"For a lousy fifty cents?!" I said. "That doesn't seem like much."

"Back then, fifty cents was a lot of money. It was enough to buy a movie ticket," he said.

"Anyway, my friend Billy beat me to it and took Stinky up on the dare. That day after gym class, Stinky peeled off one of his socks and handed it to Billy."

"You've got to be kidding, Grandpa. He really put someone's dirty old sock in his mouth?"

"This wasn't just any old sock either. I never saw a grosser-looking sock in my entire life. Not only was the sock stinky and dirty but it also had a hole in the toe and the heel. The toe hole had a brown stain around it that looked like it could have been blood from a broken blister. And the worst part was it had all kinds of *stuff* sticking to it. It had grass and leaves stuck to it from the inside of his tennis shoe, and it looked like there was a piece of gum ground into the heel. It even had an old Band-Aid stuck to the bottom."

"Oh, pew! That's disgusting."

"Billy made sure he pulled the Band-Aid off before he reluctantly brought the sock up to his mouth. He held it there for a few seconds, getting a whiff of the nasty smell. To me the sock smelled like a mixture of rotten eggs and a dead squirrel. We were all sure he was going to give the sock back to Stinky and come to his senses, so we cheered him on, 'Go, Billy! Do it! Do it!'

"He slowly pushed that dirty old thing in his mouth. First the top of the sock with the red and blue stripe and what looked like a coffee stain or bicycle chain oil. Next came the heel with the hole and the ground-in gum. He left the front of the sock with hole in the toe hanging over his lip. Stinky made him put the whole thing in his mouth or the bet was off. Billy shoved the rest of it in and nervously waited the sixty seconds so he could collect his pay.

"Oh, man, that had to be nasty! Did he do it?"

"Yup, he made it the whole sixty seconds and earned his fifty cents, but he got so sick that he missed the next three days of school."

I looked at my grandpa and shook my head. "That wasn't only the biggest dare, Grandpa, it was also the dumbest."

Easter Games

I can't remember how old I was when I stopped believing in the Easter Bunny; but it doesn't matter cuz I still get two Easter baskets every year, one from my mom and dad (the Easter Bunny) and one from my grandma (the other Easter Bunny). Every year we go over to my grandpa and grandma's for dinner, and my grandma always says, 'You kids better look around because I think the Easter Bunny may have left you a basket at our house.' Sure enough, sooner or later we would find an Easter basket.

Grandpa must have been the one to hide the baskets, cuz the older we got, the harder it was to find them. A couple of years ago, my grandpa made us work even harder to find our baskets. He wrote out clues we had to follow in order to find the baskets. The first clue would tell us to go upstairs and look under the bed. When we looked under the bed, there was another clue; and it said go in the basement and look by the pool table; and the note there said to look back upstairs by the couch . . . and on and on. We must have gone up and down those steps twenty times before we finally found our baskets.

The best part about going to my grandpa and grandma's on Easter was the Easter egg hunt and the games my grandpa made up that we would play. When we were little, we always did some kind of egg hunt. The eggs would have candy and coins in them. My brother and sister and I would always see who could get the most money.

When we got bigger, my grandpa had to think up different games instead of an egg hunt, and each year the game would get harder. One year, he had us run around the house with an egg on a spoon. He said if the egg fell off the spoon and didn't break, you could pick it up and put it back on the spoon and keep going. But if the egg broke, you were out of the race. Half-way around the house my egg fell off the spoon and broke. The same thing happened to my brother. But my sister's egg fell off three times and didn't break, so she made it all the way around the house and won. We found out later that my grandpa gave my sister a hard-boiled egg and that's why hers didn't break.

Another year, my grandpa took one hundred pennies and dropped them all over his front yard in the grass. Then he gave each of us a basket and said whoever found the most pennies won the golden egg. Of course, the golden egg had some special prize in it. This was a great idea and lots of fun, except we couldn't find very many pennies.

Eventually each of us got to pick one adult to help us find the pennies, but that still didn't do much good cuz they couldn't find the pennies either. My Grandma finally told everyone it was time for dinner, so we had to quit looking. The total number of pennies that everyone found was only sixty-seven. That meant there were still thirty-three pennies hiding in the grass that nobody ever found.

Grandpa said he would never play that game again—not cuz he lost thirty-three pennies but cuz, all summer long, when he was cutting the grass in the front yard, he kept hitting pennies with the power mower, making them come flying out. One flew out and hit the big white bear Grandpa has in his front yard. It took off a piece of the bear's nose. Another one put a small hole in the next-door neighbor's siding, and another one flew out and hit a parked car on the other side of the street. Grandpa said he had to start wearing long pants when he cut the grass cuz sometimes the pennies would hit him in the legs. He said one of the pennies hit him so hard it left an imprint of Abraham Lincoln's face right on the side of his leg . . . but I didn't believe that.

The next year, my grandpa decided to include some of the adults in the games. We did the three-legged-race, but that turned out to be a scam cuz Uncle Tim got paired up with my little sister. When the race started, my sister just wrapped her whole body around my Uncle Tim's leg, and he just sort of ran down to the finish line like she wasn't even there. Cheaters!

The final game was supposed to be the water balloon toss, but Grandma put a stop to that cuz it was too cold out. So Grandpa changed it to an egg toss instead. My sister, Tate (the cheater), played the game with my older cousin, Jesse, who was in college.

Jesse and my sister were doing pretty good, and it looked like they might win. On their last throw, Jesse threw the egg pretty high in the air and my sister screamed as the egg was coming down. She had both hands straight up in the air to catch the egg, but at the last second she got scared and tried to get out of the way of the flying egg. She was too slow, and the egg hit her on the top of the head.

The egg ran down the front of her face, and the yolk made her look like she was a circus clown with a yellow nose. It got all over her hair and on her new Easter dress. We all started laughing, and she ran in the house crying to Grandma. Grandma came out hollered at Grandpa for playing such a stupid game, and I think that was the last year we ever played games for Easter.

The State Fair

Our family went to the State Fair yesterday and we had a pretty fun time, except we had to leave early cuz my sister threw up on her shoes. I couldn't understand why we had to leave just cuz she had puke on her shoes. When we first got to the fair, my dad stepped in a fresh pile of horse manure, and we didn't have to leave cuz he had horse poop on *his* shoes. When I asked my mom what the difference was, she said, "Because your dad doesn't care if he smells like the back end of a horse. Besides, your sister is sick, that's the difference."

I told my sister not to eat so many cheese curds but she wouldn't listen. I don't really like cheese curds too much cuz they look pretty nasty; but I have to admit, they look better in the little basket before you eat them than they did on my sister's shoes after they'd been in her stomach.

The next day, I went to visit my grandpa and told him what happened. He said he couldn't remember ever throwing up at the fair, but he remembered stepping in horse poop . . . well, he didn't actually step in it, his brother pushed him and he fell backwards and sat in it. My grandpa said it was a good thing it wasn't very fresh. Then he told me a couple of stories about the fair.

"When I was your age, my brother, David, and I got to go to the fair every day because our dad worked at the fair."

"Every day? No way!" I said.

"Yup, our dad was a mounted policeman, and he would sneak us into the fair by having us hide under a blanket in the back of the car. The mounted policemen would ride their horses around the fence line and try to catch people that were climbing over the fence to sneak in so they wouldn't have to pay. One time my dad caught a ninety-year-old lady trying to sneak in. She didn't actually try to climb over the fence. Her grandson cut a big hole in the fence with a pair of cutters; and when she crawled through the hole, my dad caught her."

"Wait a minute, Grandpa! Your dad was supposed to *stop* people from sneaking into the fair. But he snuck the two of you in every day?"

"I know. I know it doesn't seem right. But for some reason back then, it just seemed okay. Anyway, my brother and I would water, feed, and brush down the mounted policemen's horses. If we finished early enough, sometimes we would get to ride the horses before the Mounties went to work. David was too small for his feet to fit in the stirrups; so whenever he rode one of the horses, he would bounce in the saddle like a basketball. One time the horse he was riding went kind of fast, and David bounced right out of the saddle onto the ground. He scraped up his face pretty good. But I told him he'd better not cry or else we might not get to ride the horses anymore, maybe not even get to come to the fair.

"My brother was pretty smart for his age—sometimes he could be a little smart-aleck—but more than once his smartness paid off for us. We didn't have any money, so every morning we would sell newspapers. That way we had some money to spend in the afternoon."

"How much money would you make?" I asked.

"We got five cents for every paper we sold. If we could each sell twenty papers in the morning, we would each have a dollar to spend in the afternoon—that was a lot of money back then. We used to love to just walk around and smell the food. Our favorite place to eat was the fifteen-cent hamburger joint. As soon as we got paid for our papers, we would hurry over to the hamburger joint, and each of us would get two hamburgers and an order of fries. Since our family almost never got to eat at a restaurant, and there were no such places as McDonalds or Burger King, we were in seventh heaven with our fifteen-cent burgers."

"They didn't have McDonalds when you were a kid, Grandpa? Wow! You must really be old."

"Don't get smart, little one, or you won't get to hear my State Fair stories."

"I'm just kidding, Grandpa, you know that." I could tell my grandpa wasn't really mad cuz he was sort of laughing when he said it.

Then Grandpa told me the three places at the fair they liked best were: Machinery Hill, the stock car races and the Midway. He said that most days they would either go pretend to drive the tractors on Machinery Hill or go to the Midway. Once in a while, their dad could sneak them into the grandstand so they could watch the stock car races. Grandpa said they loved that, but they always wanted to see the big Labor Day race because it was really long and there were lots of accidents. But for some reason, their dad could never sneak them into that race.

"So you never got to see the Labor Day race?"

Grandpa answered, "I didn't say that. I said my dad couldn't sneak us into the Labor Day race. Since the Labor Day race was a really long one, sometimes the people would come out of the grandstand for awhile and walk around. Then they would show their ticket stub to the guy at the gate, and he would let them back into the race. That's when my brother, David, came up with an idea. We both walked up to the guy at the exit gate. David told the guy we lost our ticket stubs when we came out but could we get back in? The guy just looked at us and said, 'Nobody gets back in without a ticket stub, now get lost.'

"Then I came up with a better idea. I told David, 'All

we have to do is ask someone who is leaving if we can have their ticket stub.' David asked this one guy for his stub, but the guy was kind of grumpy and told him no. Then I saw this older couple leaving, and I put on the charm. I told the lady that I wanted to bring the ticket stubs to school for show-and-tell. I said I had collected lots of other souvenirs from the fair and was going to put them all together and make a project out of them. It turned out the lady used to be a teacher and thought that was such a good idea that she not only gave me the two ticket stubs but she even gave me the program she had bought. We took the ticket stubs to one of the gates, and they let us in. We were able to watch the last two hours of the race."

"That was pretty sneaky, Grandpa," I said.

"Most days we went to the Midway—you know, where they had the rides and games and freak shows."

"Freak shows!" I said, "I didn't see any freak shows when we were at the fair yesterday. What kind of freak shows are you talking about?"

"They used to have this great big tent in the middle of the Midway with signs all over it showing all the *freaks* of nature. There was the alligator man, and the bearded lady, the leopard lady, and the world's tiniest lady, and the lobster lady who had a claw for one of her arms."

"Are you serious, Grandpa, an alligator lady and a lobster lady? No way!"

"They were all a scam, but you had to pay fifty cents to find that out. The leopard lady just had dark spots on her back, and the alligator man had some kind of skin problem so his arms and legs were all scaled. I don't think we ever saw the lobster lady."

"But you paid fifty cents to see them, Grandpa?"

"Not a chance. David and I weren't about to waste our money on something that stupid. When we sold papers in the morning, we would go to the trailers where the people who were supposed to be the freaks stayed. And that's how we saw them. One afternoon we went around to the back of the freak-show tent and found a place where we could sneak under the side. When we got inside, we found ourselves in the bearded lady's dressing room."

"Really! In her dressing room!" I said. "Did you get in trouble?"

"No, we got lucky. At first she was a little mad and was going to turn us in. Then we started talking to her, and she turned out to be a pretty nice lady. She didn't really have a full beard like the picture on the tent. She just had some long hairs growing under her chin and on her neck. It looked pretty creepy. Anyway, she pointed to a curtain and told us, if we crawled under it, we could see the whole show and nobody would bother us, so we did."

"The other thing we liked to do in the Midway was watch the suckers lose their money at the games."

"It's the same way at the fair today, Grandpa. I saw lots of people spending their money trying to win these HUGE stuffed animals, but I sure didn't see very many people who had won one."

"I know. That's because every game in the Midway is rigged in one way or another. Sometimes David would stand there for hours trying to figure out how a game was rigged. We knew they were rigged; we just didn't know how. One day David figured out how the Coke bottle game was rigged, and he told me he was going to beat it."

"What's the Coke bottle game?" I asked.

"Well, in that game the operator leans a coke bottle against a board. Then he gives you a fork and tells you all you have to do is stand the coke bottle up with the fork, and if it stays up and doesn't tip over, you win."

"Sounds pretty easy to me," I said.

"It sounds pretty easy to everyone. That's why so many suckers lose their money on that game. David told me they give you as many free tries to do it as you want and the bottle never tips over; but as soon as you give them your money and try it, the bottle tips over. He figured the guy must set the bottle up a certain way for your free try, and that's why it stays up; then, when you give him your money, he turns the bottle a different way and the bottle won't stay up. David said he did it three times and it stayed up.

"I asked David how he planned to win. He said he was going to wait until there were a lot of people around and then ask the guy for a free try. When the guy set the bottle up for the free try, David said he was going to put his quarter on the counter and say, 'Here's my money,' and then stand the bottle up."

"Wow, Grandpa, that sounds cool. Did it work?"

"Let me finish. I went with David to the Coke bottle game to watch him win his big bear. David went through each step just as he planned. The guy at the booth even told David that, if he won, he could have the biggest bear they had because it was Kids' Day. After the guy set David's bottle up for the free try, David waited until the guy went over to help someone else, then put his money on the counter and yelled 'Here's my money!' When he stood the Coke bottle up, the guy in the booth hadn't even realized David put his money on the counter. David hollered, 'I won! I won!' and all the people cheered.

"The guy came over to David and wasn't very happy, but he said, 'Okay, kid, which one of those little bears do you want?' My brother started to throw a fit because the guy told him before that he could have the biggest bear in the place if he won. Now he was trying to tell David he could only have the little bear. The guy kept saying, 'Read the sign, kid. It says you have to win twice to win the big bear.' David hollered back at him, 'You told me because it was Kids' Day I only had to win once. It's not fair. You said I'd get the big bear if I won today.'"

"Your brother must have been pretty brave to say all that to the guy . . . or pretty stupid. What happened?"

"Just wait, it gets better. All the people that were at the booth started to get upset with the guy in the booth. They all hollered, 'Give the kid the big bear! He earned it!' Then David got really smart and said, 'If you don't let me have the big bear like you said you would, I'm going to tell all these people how this game works.' So the guy finally gave David the big bear."

"Did David tell all the people how the game worked?" I asked.

"No, David got his big bear, and when the people asked him how it worked, he said. 'I was just making that up.' That David was a pretty smart kid."

Grandpa's Crazy Ideas

I was going through my book today and decided I needed a whole chapter on just the crazy ideas my grandpa came up with for me and Cole to do. The reason I'm doing this is cuz my grandpa says, if you want to be a good writer, sometimes you've got to "mix things up a little to hold the reader's interest." Well, I'm not exactly sure what that means, but this is my way of mixing things up.

This first one will show you just how dumb my grandpa's ideas can be. Actually, it was kind of fun but a really dumb idea. It was a nice sunny day in the middle of November, and my brother and I and my friend Drew rode our bikes to my grandpa's house. Even though it was sunny, it was still only about thirty degrees, so it wasn't very warm. When we got to Grandpa's, he was cleaning out some boxes in the garage and had found a bag of balloons.

Right away my grandpa said, "I got an idea. Let's make some water balloons and play a game." Cole, Drew and I looked at Grandpa like he was crazy. Didn't he realize it was freezing outside and that you're supposed to throw water balloons in the summer?

Then Grandpa told us what he wanted to do. He said one person would get on his bike and ride down the street while the rest of us would try to hit the person on the bike with a water balloon. Then the next person would try it, and so on, and so on. Everyone would have to take a turn riding the bike. The balloon throwers would have to stay in the middle of the yard to throw the water balloons; that way, it wouldn't be very easy to hit the person on the bike.

Well, it was kind of fun, but Grandpa was wrong about it being hard to hit someone from the middle of the yard. When it was my turn to ride down the street, I got hit by three water balloons and got soaked. Cole got hit twice. Drew also got hit twice, once on the top of his head. Grandpa was either the best rider or the luckiest cuz he never really got hit at all. One of the water balloons hit his bike and splashed water on his socks, but everyone else got hit by at least two balloons. Of course, Grandpa got to go in the house and change though he wasn't even very wet, but we had to ride our bikes home in the cold while we were soaking wet. Drew thought my grandpa was crazy; and when we got home, my mom didn't think it was very funny at all. She said that, if either one of us got sick, Grandpa would be in big trouble.

My next story is another cold one. About ten years ago, my grandpa built a sauna in his basement. When Cole and I were little (about three and four years old), we used to go in the sauna with my grandpa. Then, after we would get really hot and sweaty, he would let us pour a bucket of ice-cold water all over him. But the catch was he got to pour a bucket of ice-cold water on us first.

When we got a little older, my grandpa said we could do a "polar bear" with him. When we asked him what a polar bear was, he said, "That's when we get all hot and sweaty in the sauna then go outside and roll in the snow."

We thought that sounded pretty cool. The first couple of times we did it, my brother and I would just run outside, sit down in the snow and then run back into the sauna. My grandpa told us we weren't doing a true polar bear unless we rolled in the snow and covered ourselves with it.

After a while, my brother and I got pretty good at it. We would have contests to see who could roll down the hill the furthest or stay in the snow the longest. When there was a lot of snow, we'd see who could bury himself the deepest. My grandpa would do the contests with us, but he would always be the first one to go in. So he never won.

Whenever we did a polar bear, it was always dark, so we would do it in our boxer shorts. My grandpa said, when he used to do a polar bear up north at his friend's cabin, everybody did it in their birthday suits. I wasn't sure what a birthday suit was, so I asked my brother, and he said that meant they did it naked. Grandpa said we couldn't do it in our birthday suits here cuz the neighbors might be looking out their windows, and he didn't want them calling the cops cuz we were running around naked.

One time, when we were seeing who could stay buried in the snow the longest, I got my brother good. Grandpa ran in the house first, as always, and I went in next. Cole was still in the snow when I went in, so I locked the door on him. He pounded on the door, but Grandpa couldn't hear him cuz he was already down in the basement in the sauna.

When I got in the sauna, my grandpa asked where my brother was, and I said he must still be in the snow. After a couple of minutes, my grandpa went upstairs to see if anything had happened to Cole. When he walked up the stairs, he heard the doorbell ringing and pounding at the front door. It was Cole. He was really mad. "Luke locked the back door so I couldn't get in, and I've been running around the house in my boxer shorts trying to get in," Cole said. "The people across the street are probably calling the police right now and telling them there's a kid running around outside in his underwear."

When Cole and Grandpa came back downstairs, Cole started to holler at me, and I tried to act like I didn't know what he was talking about. But I couldn't keep from laughing. So Cole turned on the cold water and tried to squirt me with it; but I sat by Grandpa, so if he squirted me then he would get Grandpa. After a couple of minutes of us hollering back and forth at each other, my grandpa finally said that, if we didn't stop arguing and fighting, he was going to bring us both outside and lock all the doors, and then we'd have to walk home in our boxer shorts, and wouldn't that look cute? We were all quiet for about thirty seconds. Then Cole said, "Let's go out and do another polar bear."

This last story is the coldest of all and took place on Thanksgiving Day. Every year, we always go to my grandpa and grandma's for Thanksgiving dinner. This one year, my grandpa got this bright idea to go for a run down to White Bear Lake and jump in before dinner. Kari (that's my mom) would be at the lake waiting for us with the van; so when we got out of the lake, she could drive us back to Grandpa's where we could warm up in the sauna.

At first, my brother and I said, "No way! The lake is too cold, and we'll freeze to death." But then my grandpa said everybody would put in five dollars and the last person out of the lake would take the pot. I'm not a real math wizard, but let's see: me, Cole, my dad, Grandpa, Uncle Matt and Uncle Tim . . . that's six people. I could make thirty bucks for just jumping in the lake for a few seconds. I said I was in, and so did everyone else.

The thing I forgot about was how cold it can sometimes be on Thanksgiving Day. That morning we all got to Grandpa's at about 11:00 AM, and it was freezing. I mean it was *really* freezing. It was only eighteen degrees outside. I was only wearing running shorts and a long-sleeved T-shirt and I noticed that my knees were starting to turn red. My grandma gave me a pair of gloves so my hands wouldn't freeze. I didn't even care that the gloves were bright pink cuz they kept my hands warm.

It was almost two miles from my grandpa's house to the lake; so by the time we ran to the lake, we would all be pretty hot and sweaty. I was beginning to wonder if this was such a good idea, since I noticed some of the ponds by my grandpa's house had ice on them. I started to hope that maybe the lake would be frozen over so we wouldn't be able to jump in it. I kept thinking, *This is really a crazy idea. Only my grandpa would think of something so dumb.*

We made up the rules when we put our five dollars in the pot. First, everyone had to go in the lake at the same time. We would all line up at the edge of the lake and say *go*, and if you didn't go right in the lake, you were disqualified. Second, you could only wear a swimsuit or a pair of boxer shorts. No shoes, socks, hat, gloves, T-shirt, or anything else. And finally, you had to go completely under the water or it didn't count. The last one to get up out of the water was the winner.

As we got close to the lake, we noticed there was a little bit of ice by the shore, but the lake wasn't frozen. My grandpa saw the ice and said he wanted his money back and to drop out of the contest. Everyone told him "no way," so he started to take off his running clothes like everyone else. As we took off our clothes, we could see clouds of steam coming off our bodies from the hot sweat. I tried to convince everyone that my running shorts were a swimsuit, but that didn't work. I had to strip down to my boxers like everyone else.

We all lined up on the shore, and my dad said, "Go." As we ran into the water, my teeth were chattering, and my knees were knocking. I was already freezing, and my feet were the only part of my body that was in the water.

My brother, Cole, was the first to go all the way under, then my dad. My two uncles and I were next. Grandpa never really made it completely under the water. He ran until the water was up to his knees, dropped in, and then screamed so loud the sea gulls on the dock flew away. He immediately got out of the water and ran into the van.

When I dropped in the water and felt how cold it was, suddenly the thirty dollars didn't seem so important. I only waited about five seconds then jumped up and followed my grandpa. At least I wouldn't be the first one out of the water. I must have come up a little too fast cuz my boxers dropped down to my knees. I was too cold to try and pull them up. I just kept on running for the van, my boxers dropping lower with each step. My two uncles were right behind me, laughing. They must not have cared about the thirty bucks either.

My dad and Cole stayed in that freezing water for almost a minute before Cole finally couldn't take it anymore. When he got out of the water, he didn't move nearly as quickly as the rest of us had done. His legs were snow white, but he didn't scream. I sort of wondered if maybe he was partially frozen. My dad followed right behind him and he looked pretty much the same. When they got in the van and we headed to Grandpa's sauna, they both had purple lips, and their teeth were chattering. It was not a pretty sight.

My mom hollered at Grandpa and said this was one of the dumbest ideas he ever came up with; and if either one of her boys got sick, Grandpa would be in big trouble. When we got to Grandpa's house, my grandma hollered at Grandpa, too, and said pretty much the same thing that my mom did. I couldn't figure out why everyone was mad at Grandpa and not the rest of us, since we all jumped it the lake. Grandpa just smiled and didn't say anything.

My Ending

Since my grandpa has told me all of his stories about when he was a kid and when he was in the Navy and other stories about my dad, and I've told all the stories I can remember about my Grandpa, I guess I'm pretty much finished with my book.

In art class yesterday, I was telling my friend Leaky Jane about my book, and she thought it was pretty cool that I could write a whole book. Her real name is Janelle, but my friends call her Leaky Jane cuz she has this sinus problem that makes her nose leak, and she doesn't even know when it's going to happen. At first when they called her that, I got kinda mad cuz she's actually a really nice girl, and I didn't think she would like being called that name. But one day she told me it didn't bother her. I still won't call her that, but I don't get mad at my friends if they do.

Anyway, about her leaky nose, one time my friend Jonny was showing her the medal he won in a hockey tournament, and her nose leaked right on the medal. She tried to wipe off the medal, but it was around Jonny's neck. He was trying to get the medal off while she was trying to wipe the snot off it, and it really looked funny.

Another time in art class, we were supposed to do a water color painting. The teacher hadn't given us the water for our paint yet cuz he was still talking. Leaky Jane's nose leaked right in one of the paint containers, so she just picked up her brush and started painting with the drips of snot.

But the best time her nose leaked was in our science class. We were working on a science project with some kind of bicarbonate in a test tube. Leaky Jane was my partner. The teacher was telling us that this was a very special kind of bicarbonate, and it would only take one very small drop of water to activate it. While he was talking, Leaky Jane accidentally dripped two big drops of snot in the test tube, and the bicarbonate started to bubble all over the place. The teacher sent me and Leaky down to the office cuz he thought we spit in our test tube. We had a hard time convincing the principal that it was her nose leaking that got us in trouble.

But anyway, she's actually a really good artist (for a sixth grader), and she asked me if I wanted her to make some pictures or sketches to go with the book. I told her I'd have to think about it and let her know later. I was going to talk to my grandpa about it and see what he says, but then I decided not to. I don't think I want a girl drawing a picture of me in my boxer shorts while I'm rolling around in the snow or coming out of the lake, even if she is my friend. My grandpa has given me a lot of good advice about my book, but this is one decision I think I'm going to make on my own.

A couple of my friends thought it was pretty stupid to do all this writing. They said it was a lot of wasted time cuz I could have been out playing soccer or riding my bike or other cool stuff like that, instead of just sitting around writing stuff down on paper. Part of me agrees with them, a little. There were times when I was writing that it got kind of boring, like when I had to write about my goofy sister. And there were times when it wasn't all that fun, like when my mom made me correct the spelling errors. I wasn't too crazy about her showing me my mistakes. But it's a good thing she did, cuz I had one error that could have been embarrassing.

When she read the part about baseball in our backyard, she said, "Do you really want to say this, Luke?"

I asked her what she meant, and she said, "Well, in this sentence, I *think* you meant to say, 'We couldn't believe Cole's hit.' But the 's' after Cole's name ended up next to the word 'hit.' So guess what it says?"

I wrote the words "Cole's hit" on a piece of paper, and

then moved the "s" next to the word hit. When I read it, I turned all red in the face and fixed that mistake right away. Sometimes Moms can be helpful.

I've had a couple of my friends ask me what I'm going to do with the book, now that I've finished writing it. They also wanted to know if I'm going to keep writing. My friend Leaky Jane said maybe I should write a sequel and call it "DIARY OF A FUNNY LUKE" like that one book that's out. But I don't think I'm as funny as my grandpa, so I probably won't do that. Maybe next year I'll write some stuff for the school paper, as long as I don't have too much homework.

The most important thing about this whole project was this: by doing it, I got to learn a lot of really interesting, funny, clever things about my grandpa that I never knew before, and I also found out some pretty neat stuff about my family. Another thing I thought was pretty cool was, whenever Grandpa and I did something that made my mom and dad mad, he was the one who got in trouble, not me. Oh yeah, there is one more thing. I'll probably never, ever say "me and Grandpa" again . . . it's "Grandpa and I."

I guess if you were to ask me if I would recommend writing a book to my friends, I'd have to say sure . . . as long as theirs doesn't turn out to be better than mine.

25138301R10082

Made in the USA
San Bernardino, CA
20 October 2015